The Kind of Friends We Used to Be

Also by Frances O'Roark Dowell

The Kind of Friends We Used to Be

by Frances O'Roark Dowell

SCHOLASTIC INC.

New York   Toronto   London   Auckland
Sydney   Mexico City   New Delhi   Hong Kong

ACKNOWLEDGMENTS

The author would like to acknowledge the following people: Lizzy and Barbara Dee, for their help with word choices and titles and for their overall enthusiasm for this project; Sujata Kishnani, for her many title suggestions; Pastor Frank Venable, for providing an excellent role model for certain fictional pastors; Kiley Fitzsimmons, for her editorial insights and kind words; and for Beth Sue Rose, who has always felt sure Kate and Marylin had a story to tell and who has worked so hard to get that story to as many kids as possible.

The author would also like to acknowledge the usual suspects, who continue to tolerate her silly idiosyncrasies and give her life meaning: Amy Graham; Kathryn and Tom Harris; Danielle Paul; the O'Roarks; the Dowells; the marvelous Jonikas girls; and of course, and especially, Clifton, Jack, and Will (and Travis, too).

ISBN 978-0-545-29356-3

12 11 10 9 8 7 6 5 4 3 2 1   10 11 12 13 14 15/0

Printed in the U.S.A.   40

First Scholastic printing, September 2010

Book design by Sonia Chaghatzbanian
The text for this book is set in Lomba Book.

For Caitlyn M. Dlouhy,
the most fabulous editor ever and
a friend beyond compare

play guitar

When Kate decided to play the guitar, she realized she would need new shoes. All her life she had worn gym shoes, running shoes, soccer cleats, hiking boots, and red Chuck Taylor high-tops, whatever kind of sports shoe made the most sense at the time. Her mother didn't even bother buying her dress shoes anymore. A woman she worked with had a daughter with Kate's exact shoe size who they could borrow from in cases of emergency, such as Kate's second cousin Janice's wedding this past July.

But as a future guitar player, Kate had new wardrobe responsibilities. She knew this from watching the girl guitar players on MTV2 over at Marcie Grossman's house. She wasn't allowed to watch MTV2 or regular MTV or any show that was remotely interesting at her own house, so she had to go to Marcie's to get caught up on significant cultural events. The week before there had been a special on girls with guitars, and watching it Kate got this flying feeling, like she had just discovered a new continent, one where you could say what you wanted or be who you wanted as long as you were holding a guitar. This was her continent, Kate decided. This was where she belonged.

There were at least two kinds of girl guitar players, Kate noted. There was, for instance, the retro girl guitar player. This was not Kate's type. Kate didn't wear 1950s prom dresses, or makeup, and platform shoes or sandals with spiked heels were completely out of the question. She'd tried making pouty faces in the mirror, but mostly she looked like she was going to throw up.

But there was another kind of girl guitar player. This kind wore jeans and T-shirts and, most importantly, really cool shoes. Sometimes she played acoustic guitar, sometimes electric, sometimes her hair was short and spiky, sometimes it was long and hung in her face. But no matter what, this kind of guitar player girl always had shoes that made you pay attention. Big black shoes, cowboy boots, combat boots, whatever kind of shoes she wore, they were shoes that said, Don't mess with me, or, You will never be as cool as I am, so don't even try.

Kate needed shoes like this in her life.

The night before she decided to learn how to play the guitar, she'd gone to a Back-to-School party at Marylin's house. Throwing a Back-to-School party was a very Marylin thing to do, which Kate would know, since she and Marylin had been friends since preschool and had managed to stay friends, even though Marylin was now a middle-school cheerleader and cared too much about her hair.

Marylin was a big believer that life could be just the way it looked in girls' magazines, where you and all your Best Friends Forever got together before school started and made crafty decorations for your lockers and traded fingernail polish tips, like throw away any bottle you've had for more than a year. Marylin believed that life could be sparkly all the time, even if your parents had just gotten a divorce, which hers had. It just took a little extra work and some lip gloss, and life would be like a TV show everyone wanted to watch.

Marylin's party was a sleepover party, so only girls were invited for the whole thing, but boys were invited for the first half. The boys Marylin invited were not Kate's favorite type. They were boys like Wes Porter and Robbie Ballard, soccer-player boys, boys who did not talk to girls who weren't cheerleaders. In Kate's opinion, boys like this should have to do community service at nursing homes or hospitals, where people were wrinkly or covered with bandages on the outside but probably had beautiful souls. Boys like Wes Porter and Robbie Ballard did not think enough about people's souls, as far as Kate could tell.

And, it went without saying, they did not talk to girls like Kate Faber, basketball-playing girls with plain brown hair and a jungle of freckles on their noses and cheeks. So for the first two hours of the party, the hours that the boys were there, Kate had watched murder mystery shows on TV in the family room with Marylin's little brother Petey, who was about to start fourth grade and was actually pretty good company. He knew a lot about solving homicides for a nine-year-old. He kept pointing out stuff to her, like how weasely this one guy looked around the eyes, even though he was very handsome in general.

"That's how you can tell who did it," Petey had explained, his face moon-white in the TV's glow. "By looking at their eyes. People blink when they lie, so that's a big giveaway."

Kate had tried to get caught up in the shows. The room was dark except for the TV, and it was sort of cozy. If she'd been home, eating a bowl of cereal, her dog, Max, sleeping on the other end of the couch, she would have congratulated herself on finding a perfect way to spend the Friday night before school started.

But since it was Marylin's couch, and since there were fifteen people in the backyard who thought that being good-looking was the only valid reason for being alive and weren't the least bit interested in what Kate was doing or why, Kate did not feel she was having a perfect evening. She was feeling left out by people she didn't even like. It was insulting.

It occurred to her then that if she played guitar, she would not have these kinds of problems. She thought of the guitar-playing girls on TV. They didn't care about cheerleaders and soccer players and feeling left out. All they cared about was expressing themselves with their guitars and their big shoes. They were above middle school and all the stupid things that happened there, which is exactly what Kate wanted to be.

She'd gotten up early the next morning and carefully stepped over the sleeping bodies of the other party guests, mostly a bunch of skinny, soon-to-be seventh-grade cheerleaders, none of whom had paid any attention to her during the slumber party part of the party either, and headed home in her pajamas so she wouldn't wake anybody up trying to get dressed. She only lived across the street and three houses down, so if anyone saw her, they'd probably just think she was out looking for Max. What she wanted to do was go home and think about guitars. Just *thinking* about thinking about guitars made her feel better.

That early in the morning, she didn't expect to see Flannery out walking her dog, especially since she hadn't seen Flannery all summer and had halfway assumed she had moved or become a juvenile delinquent and run away. Flannery had spent most of the year before trying to ruin Kate's life by making everyone, including Marylin, treat her like dirt, but then suddenly she'd discovered eighth graders and stopped caring about Kate and Marylin altogether.

Now Flannery had hot pink hair and wore lots of eye makeup. When she saw Kate, she waved. "I like your jams," she called out. "They're exactly like you."

Kate looked down at her pajamas, a tank top and shorts, yellow cotton printed with red strawberries. How could they be exactly like her? They weren't exactly like anything, except maybe a piece of strawberry shortcake, which was nothing like Kate, who did not think of herself as sweet, or as a dessert item, for that matter.

"Why are you out so early?" Kate asked Flannery, not able to think of anything else to say. Flannery was not in her pajamas. She was wearing a black T-shirt and cut-off shorts and flip-flops. Her toenails were painted silver. She looked approximately twenty-three years old.

"My mom said if I didn't take better care of Rocko here, she was going to send him to the old dogs' home, where they'd probably wait, like, thirty seconds before putting him to sleep."

Kate tilted her head to one side and squinted, as if to better study her former enemy. She would not have pegged Flannery as the sort of person who would try to save a dog's life, especially a dog as drooly and disgusting-looking as Rocko, who clearly had a serious eye-goop problem.

Flannery hopped up onto the hood of a silver Honda Accord that did not belong to her family and pulled Rocko's leash toward her.

Rocko stumbled a few steps into the grass and then flopped down by a tire, looking relieved to be off his feet.

"So who do you have for homeroom, anyway?" she asked Kate, and then went on without waiting for Kate to answer. "I've got Shearer. I hear she's super strict and makes you stay after if you're one second late in the morning."

Kate crossed her arms over her chest. She was starting to feel self-conscious about standing in the middle of the sidewalk in her pajamas, especially as people were beginning to drive by on their way to work or the gym. "I've got Mr. Stephens," she told Flannery. "Do you know anything about him?"

"Yeah, he's okay," said Flannery, who was going into eighth grade this year, and who, Kate could tell, clearly thought of herself as an expert on all things seventh grade. "You're lucky you didn't get Mr. Meyers. He's a creep. Not to mention a moron. I had Mr. Stephens for Algebra I. Bad case of dandruff, but otherwise not a problem."

"You mean pre-algebra, right? Algebra I is

eighth-grade math." Kate had to stop herself from rolling her eyes. Leave it to Flannery to be so dumb about school.

Flannery chewed on a cuticle for a second. "Um, I'm pretty sure what math I took last year, okay? As it happens to turn out, I'm advanced at math. I bet that blows your mind, doesn't it?"

"No," Kate said lamely. So far this morning she'd had two surprises about Flannery. One, she was nice to animals. Two, she was smart. What was next? She'd spent last year secretly wishing she'd been Kate's best friend? Given that Flannery had done everything she could to turn Marylin against her, had said mean things about Kate behind her back and to her face, and had led a wildly successful silent-treatment campaign in which no one spoke to Kate for three weeks, Kate found this highly unlikely.

Flannery tugged on Rocko's leash, pulling him back toward the sidewalk. "All the sudden I'm starving," she said. "You want to come to my house for breakfast?"

Kate wasn't sure what she should count as the third surprise, that Flannery ate breakfast, or that she would actually invite Kate to come eat it with her. Both seemed equally unlikely. She leaned over to brush some grass off the bottom of her foot, wondering if she should make up an excuse not to go to Flannery's. Eating breakfast with someone was sort of personal, and she wasn't sure she wanted to get personal with Flannery. She suspected that might be a dangerous thing to do.

"My mom's making pancakes," Flannery trilled in a singsong voice. "You'll love 'em!"

"I guess so, yeah, okay." Kate shrugged. What else could she say? She was clearly dressed for breakfast, after all. Besides, Flannery was the only person besides Petey McIntosh who'd treated her like a human being in the last eighteen hours. You had to give her points for that.

Flannery hopped off the car. "Excellent. My stepdad hardly yells at all when we have company."

Great, Kate thought, following Flannery and

Rocko down the sidewalk toward Flannery's house. Just what she wanted, to be a buffer at Flannery's dysfunctional breakfast table.

It didn't occur to her until they were sitting down to eat that Flannery hadn't asked her why she was outside in her pajamas at seven o'clock in the morning.

Of course, if you were as weird as Flannery, Kate reasoned, everything in the world might seem normal to you.

Flannery's stepdad hadn't even come down for breakfast, so it had just been Flannery, Kate, Flannery's mom, and her two little brothers, Josh and Bennie. Flannery's mom was a little too happy to see Kate, if you wanted Kate's opinion. It was sort of like she thought Kate was there to rescue Flannery from a life of crime.

"I forgot how nice your mom was," Kate told Flannery after they'd eaten and were hanging out in Flannery's bedroom. It had been a long time since Kate had been here, and it looked a lot different from how she'd remembered. Last year around this time, Flannery's room had had lots of stuffed animals and pink stuff. Now the walls were still pink, but they were covered with posters of bands who looked very, very mean, like they hoped you would fall down and die that very second.

"She's okay," Flannery said. She was sitting on her bed, painting another layer of silver polish on her toenails. "I wish she'd get a job, though. She's here every single second of the day. It drives me crazy."

"My mom works part-time," Kate said. "I actually like it when she's home. She bakes a lot. I mean, baking is actually her other part-time job. She used to be a window dresser, but she decided that baking is what she really loves most of all. She does wedding cakes and cakes for parties. So it really smells good when my mom's home."

"You know, a lot of the time you talk like you're about eight years old," Flannery told her matter-of-factly, leaning forward so she could blow on her toes. "Maturity-wise, I mean."

Okay, this show was definitely over. The

night before she'd been ignored, this morning she was being insulted. Kate stood up to leave. She turned toward the door, and as she did she noticed Flannery's open closet door. There was no way in the world she could keep herself from looking inside it. The floor was a jumble of shoes. All the shirts were hanging halfway off their hangers. And in the middle of all the mess, leaning against the closet's back wall, was a guitar.

An electric guitar.

"Do you play that?" Kate had to know. Was Flannery, in fact, a girl guitar player who knew the secret of how to get through life without caring about anything?

"A little," Flannery told her, walking over from her bed to grab the guitar from the closet. "I mean, I know all the chords, but I'm still learning to do barre chords, which is what you have to know if you're going to be in a band."

"You're going to be in a band?" Kate asked, thinking that would explain all the eye makeup.

Flannery sat on the floor and cradled the

guitar in her lap. "Maybe. Megan Woods and I have been talking about it. Her brother is a drummer, and he said he'd let us use his drums." She looked up at Kate. "Why? Do you want to be in a band?"

"I was just thinking I might want to learn how to play guitar. It seems like it would be a fun thing to know how to do."

"That's what I mean," Flannery said, shaking her head sadly. "That is such an eight-year-old thing to say. Playing guitar isn't a fun thing to do. It's a way of life."

Kate looked at the floor. "I know that," she said quietly. "That's what I really meant."

Flannery didn't say anything for a minute, until finally she looked at Kate and nodded her head. "I believe you," she said. "I believe that's what you really meant."

And then she handed Kate the guitar. "Take it," she said. "Borrow it for a few days. Take the amp, too."

Kate stared at the guitar for a moment. It felt so natural, the way her left hand fit around the neck, the curve of the body resting in her right hand. "No, I couldn't," she said reluctantly. "I mean, I can't borrow something this important."

"It's no big deal," Flannery said. "My dad says he's going to get me a new one."

"Really?" Kate asked. "Are you serious? I can borrow this?"

"I've never been more serious about anything in my entire life."

Kate looked at Flannery.

She believed her.

When Marylin called that afternoon, Kate was busy playing the E-minor chord. In addition to the guitar and amplifier, Flannery had also lent her a book about how to teach yourself to play guitar, and Kate was going through it page by page, looking for the really easy stuff. In Kate's opinion, E minor sounded great.

"Where did you go this morning?" Marylin asked. "When I woke up and didn't see you there, I was worried sick."

"So how come you're only calling me now? It's after lunch." Kate strummed another E minor, which sounded satisfyingly dramatic and sad at the same time.

"Well, it took forever to eat breakfast, because Mazie kept burning the pancakes, and one time the smoke alarm went off, and that made everything completely crazy. And to be honest, it wasn't until about eleven o'clock that I realized you were missing."

"That makes me feel great," Kate said. "You have no idea how much you've just improved my self-esteem."

Marylin didn't say anything for a minute. Kate could practically hear her thinking. Then she gasped and cried out, "You're right, Kate! You're right. That's awful that I didn't notice earlier! It's just with everyone running around all over the house, and the alarm going off, well, I guess I must have thought you were in the bathroom or something."

For three hours? Kate wanted to ask. But she didn't. Because from her twelve years' experience of being alive, she knew that very few people could admit they were wrong the way that Marylin just had. It was a trait you didn't want to squash out with a sarcastic remark.

"Anyway," she told Marylin, flipping through the guitar book to find another easy chord, "I just decided to come home. You were the only person there who's actually my friend."

"That's not true!" Marylin exclaimed. Then she was quiet again for a moment. "Okay, well, maybe it's sort of true. But you're friends with Ashley. You've been friends with Ashley since kindergarten."

Kate rolled her eyes. The problem with being friends with Marylin was that she was such an unrealistic person. She thought cheerleaders and regular people could be friends. True, Kate and Ashley had been friends before Ashley had become a middle-school cheerleader. In fourth grade they had done a science project together, where they used Play-Doh to show the different layers of the earth, brown for the crust, yellow for the mantle, orange for the outer core, and red for the inner core. They'd spent an entire Saturday afternoon at Ashley's house constructing the layers and making an interesting-to-look-at presentation.

Ashley's mom brought in snacks and lemonade, and her little brother kept stealing bits of Play-Doh to make a *Star Wars Millennium Falcon.*

That's what killed Kate about middle school. You could share a history with a person, know their mom and their little brother and what kind of laundry detergent they used (in Ashley's case, her family used Mountain Fresh Tide, which smelled a million times better than the baking-soda brand Kate's mom bought), but the second that person became a middle-school cheerleader, forget it. It's like all that stuff never existed.

It was different with Marylin, of course. But that's because Marylin was the sensitive type. She was the sort of person who got mad if you picked up a daddy longlegs by one of his spindly legs. "You're hurting him!" she'd yell, like the daddy longlegs was a person. True, she and Flannery had given Kate the silent treatment in sixth grade, a memory that still made Kate go cold all over, but in the end she and Marylin had become friends again. Now their friendship had cracks in places, like a vase that had fallen off a shelf and had to be glued back together. But Kate had a theory: Maybe cracks could make a friendship stronger. Cracks said, *We don't fit together a hundred percent, but that's okay.*

"What's that noise?" Marylin asked. "Do you have the radio on?"

Kate realized she'd been strumming an A chord sort of loud. It was hard not to. The A chord, which was almost but not quite as easy as an E minor, sounded so nice and happy. It sounded like the beginning of a song you'd sing to a little kid, a song about the sun coming up in the morning and the birds flying through the trees.

"I'm learning how to play guitar," she told Marylin. "It's pretty fun."

"When did you get a guitar?" asked Marylin. Kate could tell from her tone of voice that she wasn't entirely sure playing the guitar was such a great thing to do.

"Flannery lent it to me," Kate said. "I ran into her this morning."

"Is her hair still pink?"

"It's even pinker."

Marylin laughed. "Can you even believe we used to be friends with her?"

"You used to be friends with her," Kate pointed out. "Flannery and I were not friends. In fact, today was probably the second time in my life that Flannery was the least bit friendly to me."

"All I'm saying is that she's really strange." Marylin paused. "In fact, you probably shouldn't be borrowing stuff from her. You don't want people to connect the two of you together. Besides, I don't know about you playing guitar. It's sort of . . . like something a guy would do, I guess."

Marylin sounded like a school counselor or an advice columnist, someone who knew a lot about life and was there to guide you along the way.

"Girls play guitar," Kate protested. "There are lots of famous girl guitar players."

"But not in seventh grade," Marylin pointed out. "Seventh grade is a time for, I don't know, hanging out with your group of friends and getting ready for high school. It's about finding your own personal style. That's what Mazie says. She says this year we are going to focus on finding our own personal style together."

"How can finding your personal style be a group project?"

"Easy!" Marylin exclaimed, and then she began to tell Kate how each middle-school cheerleader was going to subscribe to a different fashion magazine, and every month they would gather together and look at magazines and give one another fashion tips.

Kate softly strummed an A minor, which she discovered was as easy to play as an E minor, and just as sad sounding. She liked playing guitar. She was pretty sure she was going to be good at it.

And, if she was being perfectly honest with herself—and why shouldn't she be?—she liked the idea that Marylin didn't like it. Because Marylin might have been one of Kate's best friends, but that didn't mean she knew everything in the world. In fact, in Kate's opinion,

Marylin had made some pretty poor choices. Middle-school cheerleading. Mazie Calloway. And now fashion magazine subscriptions.

In fact, sometimes Kate thought maybe she should be the one giving advice to Marylin. Drop cheerleading. Make friends with people who have good values. Ignore fashion.

Play guitar.

Kate and her mom were having a hard time agreeing on what shoes to buy.

"Let me get this straight," Mrs. Faber said, rubbing her forehead, like she felt a headache coming on. "You don't want tennis shoes for school anymore. You want those."

She pointed to a pair of black lace-up boots. They weren't combat boots exactly, but they were close to it, thick and heavy, like they were made for stomping.

Kate nodded. They were exactly what she wanted.

"But, Kate, they must weigh five pounds. They look uncomfortable. They don't go with anything you have to wear."

"They don't have to go with anything," Kate insisted. "In fact, that's what I like about them. They're like the opposite of everything I have."

Mrs. Faber took a deep breath, let it out. "It's happening, isn't it? You're turning into a teenager. I need to be calm and not panic. Living with your sister has taught me that about dealing with teenagers: Whatever you do, don't panic."

Kate's sister Tracie was fifteen. She was a little too girly for Kate's taste, with a brief cheerleading past and a dresser covered with hairspray bottles and tiny pots and tubes of makeup, all caps, tops, and lids permanently off. She had seventeen pairs of shoes and not one single thick-heeled, lace-up black boot.

"I need those boots," Kate told her mom. "They're going to be part of my new look at school this year. You want me to care what I look like, don't you? You're always bugging me to comb my hair."

"It's one thing to comb your hair," Mrs. Faber said. "It's another thing to dress like a thug, even if you're not one. Maybe especially if you're not one. What kind of fashion statement are you trying to make, Kate? 'Look at me wrong and I'll beat you up'?"

"*Mom*," Kate said, and she could hear the whine in her voice, which sounded distressingly like the whine she'd been hearing in Tracie's voice for the last three years. She decided to change tactics. Standing up straight, she said, "I'll pay for half. I've still got birthday money, plus some dog-walking money from this summer from when the Weinerts went out of town."

"You want those boots that much?"

Kate nodded. "I really do."

Mrs. Faber shrugged, then waved at a salesperson. "If you're willing to pay for half, I suppose I have no choice. But those are the only shoes I'm buying you, other than sneakers for PE. Is that understood?"

"Understood."

Until today, Kate had never gotten why shopping made people feel so happy. She'd always hated shopping, hated trying stuff on, hated having to parade around in front of her mom, who was always telling her to stand up straighter or pull her tummy in.

But now, the plastic bag with SHOEVILLE written on it in bright red letters dangling from her wrist, she felt lighter somehow, different. Could shoes really change a person's life? She was beginning to think they could.

"Let's get a lemonade, you want to?" Mrs. Faber asked. "One hour of shopping and I'm completely worn out. We'll take a little break and then go to one more place, okay? I think that's all I'm up for today."

They found a table at the food court that was only halfway covered with crumbs and spilled soda. Mrs. Faber wiped up what she could with a tissue from her purse, then went to buy their drinks. Kate sat down and opened her bag. She just wanted a little peek at her boots, just a little sniff of the shiny new leather.

"Hey there, Kate!"

Kate snatched her hand out of the Shoeville bag, like she'd been caught trying to steal something. Andrew O'Shea stood in front of her, a goofy grin on his face. "I don't know why," he said, "but I never thought I'd see you at the mall. The basketball courts, definitely. Shoeville"—he pointed at the bag—"maybe not so much."

A girl stood behind him. She was skinny and pale, with the kind of milky white skin you could see the veins underneath, like the little blue highway lines on a map. She had white blond hair, the same as Andrew, and glasses like his too.

"Is that your cousin?" Kate asked, nodding toward the girl.

"Becky?" Andrew's voice cracked on the *K* and went screeching into the *Y*. "No, Becky's my . . ." He seemed to be struggling to find the right word.

"We go together," the girl said. "We belong to the same swimming pool."

"Wow, you must get red as a lobster," Kate said before she could stop herself. "I mean," she added, trying to make it not sound like an insult, "you look like you might burn sort of easy."

The girl turned pink, but she managed to

laugh. "My dad says my skin's so white, you could lose me in a snowstorm."

Once upon a time, Kate and Andrew had almost been boyfriend and girlfriend. Actually *had* been boyfriend and girlfriend for about twenty-four hours before Kate panicked and shut the whole thing down. So she didn't know how to feel about this Becky. Should she automatically hate her? Only how could you hate a girl who was nice enough not to take an unintentionally rude remark the wrong way? Who could laugh at her own state of albino-ness?

"I got some boots," Kate told the girl. "At Shoeville. Do you want to see them?"

Becky nodded, stepping toward Kate. Kate pulled the box halfway out of the bag and opened the lid, but didn't actually take the boots out. For some reason, she wasn't ready to expose them entirely. Still, you could see what they were.

"Um, neat," Becky said, and took a step back. It was clear she did not think the boots were neat at all. It was clear she didn't get the first thing about them.

Andrew whistled. "Boys, those are some boots," he said, and for a second Kate thought that he understood. But then he shook his head. "You'll sure scare off the guys with those things."

Kate shoved the box back into the Shoeville bag. Her face felt as hot as August. "Who cares? Maybe I want to scare off guys."

Andrew put up his hands and backed away a few steps. "I'm just saying, they're not the most girly-girl shoes in the world. But, hey, that's okay. You're not really the feminine type."

Kate's throat suddenly felt tight. "Yeah, well, thanks, Andrew. I'll take that as a big compliment."

Andrew backed away a few more steps, and then he turned and, with Becky, was lost in a river of people and noise.

Kate hugged the box, still in its bag, to her chest. So what if she wasn't the feminine type. The feminine type was stupid. The feminine type giggled and pretended that everything a boy said was brilliant. The feminine type had veins you could see through her skim-milk skin, which was pretty gross, in Kate's opinion.

Mrs. Faber appeared, carrying two lemonades, two straws, and a wad of napkins. "What's wrong, Katie? You look upset."

Kate looked down at the floor. It was like a circus of straw wrappers and chewed-up chewing gum down there. "Could we just go home? I'm really tired all of the sudden."

Mrs. Faber started to say something, then stopped herself. "Sure, honey, let's go. I'm pooped too."

When they got home, Kate went to her room and closed the door. She took a fresh pair of socks out of her sock drawer and put them on. Then she took out her new boots. They were so shiny, so big. Kate thought that in their own way they were beautiful.

So she put them on.

And she played guitar.

the stars fall over

On the first day of seventh grade, Marylin woke up in a room full of sparkles and light. A magical feeling fell over her as she watched the light dancing upon her walls, and it occurred to her that maybe one of her little-girl wishes had finally come true and she had entered the land of the fairies.

As it turned out, it was her little brother Petey who had lit up the walls with practically every star in the universe. He'd set up his solar system projector while she was still sleeping, turned it on, and hummed "Mary Had a Little Lamb" until she woke up. "I thought it was a funner way to wake you up than just yelling,

'*Wake up!*'" he explained to her when she'd finally figured out that she was not, after all, in a magical fairy realm, but in her plain, ordinary room.

Marylin had felt disappointed at first, then silly. Fairies! Here she was, about to start seventh grade, and she was still imagining there were fairies.

She hoped nobody would tell Mazie she'd been that dumb.

Not that anyone else could possibly know Marylin's thoughts upon waking up first thing in the morning, but still. Mazie had a way of finding out impossible things.

After Petey took his solar system back to his room, Marylin got out of bed and began her preparations for the first day of school. She and Mazie and the other middle-school cheerleaders had spent practically the entire night before messaging each other about what they would be wearing and how they should accessorize. Makeup had also been a big topic. Mazie and Ruby Santiago and Caitlin Moore claimed they could wear as much makeup as they wanted, as long as it didn't look tacky or cheap. Marylin hadn't known if she should admit that she was limited to clear lip gloss and the tiniest bit of eye shadow. Fortunately, Ashley Greer had been brave enough to IM, 2 BAD MY MOM SEZ NO MAKEUP 4 ME. Then Marylin could message, MY MOM SEZ JUST A LITTLE IS ENUF.

A LITTLE CAN LOOK GR8, Ruby had written. B-SIDES, U DON'T NEED IT.

Of all the cheerleaders, Ruby was the nicest. Ruby was the nicest and Mazie was the meanest. So how did Marylin, who considered herself a very nice person, get stuck being best cheerleader friends with Mazie? It was like Mazie had swooped down and picked Marylin up in her claws before Marylin had had a chance to choose.

If you thought about it, Marylin should really be best cheerleader friends with Ashley Greer. Before they made cheerleader, they had both been in the middle group of girls, girls who were nice and got good report cards, girls who were not the popular girls but in the next group down. Now that they were cheerleaders, Marylin and Ashley had moved up in the ranks, leaving behind Kate and Brittany Lamb and Marcie Grossman and the other middle-group girls. They were the only middle-school cheerleaders who had not always been popular. They were the only ones whose families weren't members of New Hope Creek Country Club. Really, they had a lot in common.

But for some reason, Marylin and Ashley barely talked to each other. It felt too dangerous. It was like they didn't want to remind the others that they hadn't always been stars.

Marylin pulled on the red-and-white-striped T-shirt all the middle-school cheerleaders had decided to wear. They'd bought them at Target, where they had met the week before to go back-to-school shopping. Ruby thought it would be nice if they showed school spirit by wearing school colors on the first day of seventh grade, and Marylin had agreed, although she'd agreed quietly. Mazie thought they should buy black T-shirts that had HOT STUFF! written across the front in sparkly silver letters, and you could tell she expected Marylin to be on her side. Marylin had pretended to be checking out sunglasses during the discussion.

She'd made the mistake of telling Kate about the whole thing the next night, when they'd taken Max for a walk around the block after dinner. They'd been talking about school starting the next week, what their teachers would be like, how seventh grade would probably be different from sixth grade. Then Marylin had brought up the subject of clothes and the plan the cheerleaders had made to dress alike on the first day.

"I won't even comment on everybody dressing the same for the first day of school," Kate had said. "I won't even mention the corniness of wearing school colors on purpose when it's not Spirit Week. But wanting to buy T-shirts that say 'Hot Stuff!'—I mean, did you ever hear of not looking totally dumb the first day of school?"

"Mazie was the only one who wanted to do it," Marylin had protested. "And besides, it was just for a joke."

"I'm pretty sure Mazie Calloway thinks she's hot stuff," said Kate. "That's no joke."

"She's nicer than she seems," Marylin lied. "You just don't know her."

"Haven't we had this discussion before?" Kate said. "I don't want to know her. Don't you remember that time she completely humiliated Brittany?"

Marylin played dumb. "No, not really."

"Sure you do," Kate said, sitting down on the little hill in front of her house and yanking Max's leash to make him sit too. "She taped that note on the back of Brittany's shirt that said, 'Be nice to me, I've got my period today.' That was in fifth grade—hardly anybody had their period! I know you remember that."

Marylin sat down next to Max and scratched his ears. She did remember that, although it was something she tried not to think about. Her main memory of the event was how relieved she'd been that Brittany had been picked for the joke, not her.

"Anyway," Marylin had said, wanting to change the subject, "what are you wearing for the first day of school? Have you picked out an outfit?"

"We've got a week before school starts," Kate had pointed out. She plucked a piece of grass from the lawn and put it between her thumbs to make a whistle. "I haven't even gone clothes shopping yet."

Leave it to Kate to wait until the last minute. She'd always been that way, ever since Marylin had known her. If Halloween was Tuesday, Kate was still figuring out what her costume would be on Monday night. Book report due on Wednesday? Kate was writing it on the bus on the way to school Wednesday morning. Kate's lifestyle went against everything Marylin believed in. Marylin liked to plan ahead at least one week in advance. It made her nervous to wait to write a paper till the night before it was due. She'd have a breakdown if she waited until the morning she was supposed to hand it in.

She would never say this, but she thought Kate would be happier if she were more like Marylin. For instance, if Kate would just give a little advance thought about what she wore and how she did her hair, if she would make a wardrobe chart and see what she could mix and match, if she would make the tiniest little effort to improve herself, it would make life so much easier for her.

"I'll go shopping with you if you want," Marylin had offered. "I could help you pick out stuff that looks good on you."

Marylin was in love with that idea as soon as she came up with it. She could give Kate a makeover. She knew just what kind of jeans would look great on Kate. And it would take a little doing, but maybe she could get Kate to buy some ballet slipper flats. Kate could totally do a cute look. Not too girly, of course, because the last thing Kate was was girly. But cute and sporty? Definitely.

Kate had blown a long, piercing whistle through her blade of grass. "No thanks," she'd said, dashing Marylin's dreams to the dirt. "I already know what I want. Jeans and T-shirts. I call it the casual look. It's very me."

Marylin felt her face flush red. She didn't know why she felt so flustered, but she did.

"Kate, we're starting seventh grade. It's a chance for a whole new beginning."

"I don't need a new beginning." Kate stood up. "I'm good the way I am."

Walking back to her house, Marylin had wanted to scream. She wanted to turn around and yell at Kate, "You are not good the way you are! Boys don't like you! People are starting to think you're weird."

But of course she hadn't. You couldn't say that to someone who had been your best friend practically your entire life. Not that Kate felt much like a best friend anymore. Well, she did and she didn't. Kate and Marylin had known each other since preschool. They knew each other's Pop-Tart preferences. Twice they'd both had bad dreams on the same night: once, in second grade, after they'd watched *The Wizard of Oz* for the first time, and once the night before the big fourth-grade music recital, when they'd each had a solo. And Kate was the only one Marylin could talk to about her parents getting a divorce. Kate was irritating, but she was a good person, and she was honest.

Marylin respected that, even though sometimes it drove her crazy.

But lately Marylin felt like Kate's goal in life was to be the complete opposite of her. If Marylin said hot, Kate said cold. If Marylin said, "Let's practice different hairstyles," Kate said, "Let's cut all our hair off and be bald."

Marylin wanted to help Kate, she really did. But how could she, when Kate wouldn't let her?

I'm good the way I am. Marylin shook her head. What kind of crazy talk was that?

"Sweetie, you look gorgeous," Marylin's mother greeted her when she came down for breakfast. "And that T-shirt looks great on you. Red-and-white stripes—very cute."

Ever since her parents had gotten a divorce, Marylin's mother had been big on being supportive. One time Marylin had overheard her mom on the phone telling Mrs. Faber that she worried Marylin would get low self-esteem now that she lived in a broken home. The problem was, whenever Marylin's mom said anything nice, Marylin didn't know if she meant it or not. Did she really think Marylin's shirt was cute, or was she just saying that because she was afraid Marylin might flunk out of school now that her parents were divorced?

Marylin sat down across the table from Petey, who also had a striped shirt on, and whose hair was slicked back from his forehead with styling gel. "If you're going to use gel, don't comb your hair later," Marylin advised him. "The gel will crack if you comb it when it's dry, and it will look like you have really bad dandruff."

Petey patted his hair gingerly. "Thanks for telling me," he said. "Gretchen Humboldt says that kids start getting mean in fourth grade. They make fun of you if you're different from other people. It's classic herd mentality. That's what Gretchen says, anyway."

Marylin took a tiny bite of her scrambled eggs. Sometimes she was pretty sure she knew every opinion Gretchen Humboldt had ever held. Gretchen was the only person in Petey's class smarter than he was, and Petey was always quoting her, like she was the world's foremost authority on everything.

"Mom, I'm too nervous to eat," she said after she swallowed another forkful of eggs. "I'll drink my juice, but if I eat anything else, I think I'll throw up."

That wasn't exactly true. She didn't have the throw-up feeling. It was more of a stomach explosion feeling. Not butterflies. Butterflies were light and airy. Whatever was going on in her stomach was more like elephants stomping around.

Her mom walked into the dining room, waving a cereal bar. "At least put this in your backpack," she insisted. "You can eat it when your stomach calms down. Which it will. The first day of school makes everybody jittery."

When the doorbell rang, Marylin knew it was Kate. She and Kate had always walked to the bus stop together on the first day of school. There were two bus stops on their street, one in front of Kate's house and one on the corner five houses down from Marylin's house, almost an entire block away from Kate's. In the old days, they switched back and forth, Kate's bus stop one day, Marylin's the next. Then last year, when Marylin and Flannery were giving Kate the silent treatment, Kate always caught the bus in front of her house.

Marylin wondered if now that they were friends again, they would go back to switching back and forth. They hadn't actually discussed it yet, but she thought it might be a babyish thing to do in seventh grade. Besides, Kate was almost always late when it was her day to come to Marylin's bus stop, and it drove Marylin crazy. She liked staying on the good side of bus drivers, who were often highly irritable people and didn't care if you missed the bus or not.

This morning, though, Kate was early. Maybe she was turning over a new leaf, Marylin thought. Maybe she'd realized that Marylin's way of doing things was a really good way if you wanted happiness and low stress in your life. Maybe Kate was finally coming around. Marylin grabbed her backpack—which she had started thinking of as a back pouch, since it was rounder than a backpack and quilted with pretty red and white flowered fabric—picked up her lunch tote, which was made out of the same material, and ran for the door.

"Have a great first day!" her mom called after her. "You look fabulous!"

Did she really look fabulous, Marylin wondered as she opened the door, or was her mom hoping that if she told her she looked fabulous, Marylin wouldn't suddenly turn into Flannery and dye her hair hot pink? It was impossible to know for sure.

If Marylin had been hoping to find a transformed Kate on her front porch, she knew the minute she opened the door that she was completely out of luck. Kate was dressed in a purple T-shirt without the smallest design or stylish detail, dark jeans, and—what were those things on her feet? Horseback-riding boots? Army shoes? Whatever they were, Marylin was sure of one thing: Nobody else in seventh grade would be wearing them.

She had to force herself not to tell Kate to run home before it was too late and put on some regular shoes. She knew if she said this, Kate would never take off her boots again. They would become a permanent part of her body. So Marylin just smiled at Kate, her best fake smile, a smile that she hoped said, *I don't exactly remember your name, but I've seen you around school and I'm sure you're very nice.*

"Why are you smiling at me like that?" Kate asked. "Are you about to throw up?"

"I like your T-shirt," said Marylin brightly. "Purple's a great color on you."

The funny thing was, even though Kate rolled her eyes, Marylin was sure she saw a flash of something right before she did, a little glimpse of the inside of Kate's thoughts, which said, *Do you really think so?*

Kate cared what she looked like. Marylin was sure of it.

And for some reason this made her feel all her old best-friend feelings about Kate. Kate might act tough. She might act like she didn't care anymore what anybody thought. But Marylin knew the truth. Kate cared.

"You can roll your eyes if you want," Marylin

said as they walked down the front path toward the sidewalk. "But you really do look cute. I hate to be the one to tell you that, but it's true."

She wouldn't say a word about the boots, she decided.

Not one single word.

Marylin had become a middle-school cheerleader in April, at the tail end of sixth grade. She had never before walked into school on the first day as a full-fledged cheerleader, a person everyone else knew even if she didn't know them. She had never walked down the hallway to her locker while newly minted eighth-grade football players checked her out and smiled at her, like somehow she belonged to them.

She was not sure how she felt about eighth-grade football players smiling at her like she belonged to them. Before today, she would have said that was something she would probably enjoy a lot.

Now she wasn't exactly sure.

And for some reason, when a football player

she'd never met named Thomas Langley, the third most popular eighth-grade boy in their school, called out her name as she walked down the hall and then bumped against her hip as she passed him, she thought of Petey and his hair-gelled hair, and it almost made her feel like crying.

She had no idea why.

"There she is!" Mazie was standing by her locker at the end of the hall, surrounded by the other middle-school cheerleaders. "Marylin, get down here right now!"

Marylin turned to say good-bye to Kate, but Kate was no longer by her side. Marylin hated to admit it, especially after having just experienced such warm best-friend feelings, but she was relieved Kate was gone. Now they didn't have to say, "See you later," while not actually acknowledging that in no way would Kate be welcome at the cheerleader gathering down the hall, or that Kate would rather spend the day dancing through school in a pink polka-dotted tutu than have to say one single word to Mazie Calloway.

Walking toward her fellow middle-school cheerleaders, all of them dressed in matching red-and-white-striped shirts, it seemed to Marylin like they glowed, the way a flock of angels might glow if they landed in your front yard. Even Kate would have to admit there was something special about this group of cheerleaders, not that she'd ever say so out loud.

"We're comparing schedules," Mazie informed her as Marylin joined the group.

"Did something change?" asked Marylin, pulling her own schedule out of her back pouch. They had compared schedules endlessly the week before, e-mailing and instant messaging and calling one another at all hours of the day.

"My mom called the office yesterday and made them switch me from chorus to newspaper," Ashley Greer moaned. "Which means that I don't have B lunch anymore."

Marylin stared at her. They had spent hours coordinating it so that all the middle-school cheerleaders would have B lunch. They already knew which table they were going to sit at, and had discussed whether or not any noncheer-leaders would be allowed to sit with them. Ashley's moving to another lunch period ruined the whole plan.

"Isn't there anything you can do?" Marylin asked her. "Can't you make your mom change her mind?"

"That's what we've been talking about," said Mazie. "But Ash here says that there's no way. She's too wimpy to stick up for herself."

"That's not true!" Ashley whined. "I begged her a million times. But she says the newspaper is a much better elective for me than chorus."

Caitlin Moore leaned toward Marylin and whispered, "Her mom says why should she be in chorus when she can't sing a note?"

"Don't keep telling everyone that!" Ashley screeched. "Besides, how am I supposed to become a better singer if I'm not in chorus?"

"More importantly, how can you be a cheer-leader and not have B lunch?" Mazie asked.

Ashley paled. "Can I get kicked off the squad for having a different lunch period from every-one else?"

Ruby Santiago stepped forward. "Of course not. It's just a tradition, that's all. But maybe you can change electives next quarter. You could practice your singing and show your mom that you really love music. She might change her mind."

"Thanks, Ruby," Ashley said, sounding grateful. "That's an awesome idea."

"Somebody else will have to drop out of chorus for Ashley to get back in," Mazie pointed out. "That's not very likely."

Marylin felt an opportunity opening up before her. There were clearly two sides here. There was the supportive Ruby side and the completely nonsupportive and pretty mean Mazie side. All Marylin had to do was take a step forward and say something to Ashley like, *It will all work out, don't worry*, and she would show the world which side she was on. The nice people's side. The side that stood for friendliness and making everyone feel included. That was the side where Marylin felt she truly belonged.

She started to make her move. All she had to do was lean toward Ashley and give her a nice pat on the shoulder, say a few words. She took a breath and looked at Ashley's pale, worried face. She began to open her mouth.

But then Ashley glared at her. It was a look that clearly said, *Why don't you shut up before you even start talking?*

Marylin stepped backward, as though she'd been slapped. She tried to smile in what she hoped was a sympathetic way, even though what she really wanted to do was yank out Ashley's hair.

Clearly she would have to find another time when she could show everyone what a kind, supportive person she was. Maybe she could sit next to Ruby Santiago at lunch. She could give Ruby her Baggie of Mint Milano cookies, which she knew were Ruby's favorites. Maybe Ruby would invite her over to her house to spend the night on Saturday. It would just be the two of them, and they would discover how much they had in common. Maybe Ruby liked lying on the couch on snowy days, snuggling under a quilt her grandmother had made. Maybe she liked swimming in lakes better than in swimming pools, just like Marylin did.

Mazie reached out and grabbed Marylin's wrist, pulling her out of her daydream of friendship with Ruby Santiago. "Come on," she said, dragging Marylin away from the group. "Let's go down to the gym before the bell rings and see if any cute guys are hanging around."

Marylin followed reluctantly behind her. Somehow Mazie had done it again, claimed Marylin for her own without bothering to ask if Marylin wanted to be claimed. That didn't seem fair to Marylin, that other people could say, *You're mine* and you couldn't say, *But I don't want to be yours.*

She had a sudden, brief thought that she would like to be her own, but it disappeared in the commotion of the crowded hallway. She followed behind Mazie, halfway hoping there'd be some cute boys in the gym, halfway hoping nobody would be there at all.

"Tell me everything. I want all the gory details."

Marylin's mom sat at the kitchen table, a

plate of freshly bought chocolate chip cookies in front of her. It was her first-day-of-school tradition to leave work early so she could be there when Marylin and Petey got home. Then, at the dinner table, she'd prompt them as they told their dad about the first day of school, saying, "Now, don't forget to tell him about your class pet," or "Does Daddy know who sits two seats behind you who also goes to our church?"

Only tonight Marylin's dad would not be at the dinner table to hear all their back-to-school stories. Marylin and Petey would have to call him after dinner at his apartment, which was twenty miles and a whole universe away. She knew it would feel fakey to talk to him about school on the phone. In person, her dad was a good conversationalist, but when you talked to him on the phone you could hear the little pings his computer made as he checked his e-mail or surfed the Internet. His voice was enthusiastic—"Really!" he'd exclaim when he thought he was supposed to be excited about something you'd said, "That's great, honey!"—but you could tell he was only halfway listening.

Marylin sat down across the table from her mom and took a cookie from the plate. She wished she were better at being able to talk about stuff right away. She knew that when Petey had gotten home from school, he'd probably talked nonstop, repeated every word that had come out of Gretchen Humboldt's mouth, given a five-point presentation on the fourth-grade curriculum, and ended up with a top ten list of his fourth-grade goals. Petey was great at on-the-spot talking.

But Marylin needed time to think the day through. What surprised her was that she didn't really want to think about who sat at the middle-school cheerleading table during B lunch or the cute boy in the desk behind her in pre-algebra who kept leaning forward to crack jokes in Marylin's ear, his cool breath on her earlobe making her shiver.

No, what stayed in her mind on the first afternoon after the first day of seventh grade was a new girl named Rhetta Mayes, who sat in front of Marylin in four of her classes, including art and State History. Rhetta Mayes had dyed jet-black hair and four earrings in each ear. She wore a black blouse that was at least three sizes too big, so it looked like a very fancy super sized garbage bag, and black jeans and clunky black shoes with big silver buckles. Her skin was so white, Marylin was sure it couldn't be real. It was maybe two shades up from clown-makeup white. Rhetta Mayes was, in fact, the scariest-looking person Marylin had ever seen in her life.

As far as Marylin was concerned, seventh grade was not supposed to include people like Rhetta Mayes, people who made you feel nervous in four classes out of seven. In fact, by the time seventh period rolled around and there was Rhetta Mayes again—the same humongous fake leather black bag stuffed with who knew what (a witch hat and raggedy black dress probably) hooked over the back of her desk where it would bump into Marylin's knees the whole period, the same black eyeliner-lined eyes peering spookily out from her pale face—

Marylin was ready to head to the guidance counselor's office and request a complete schedule change. *Just keep me in B lunch,* was all she'd ask. *But get me away from Rhetta Mayes.*

Seventh period was language arts, and their teacher, Mr. Holm, made them work in pairs. They would interview each other, and for homework they would write up their interviews into reports, which they would give in front of the class the next day. "I want at least three interesting facts or stories about your partner," Mr. Holm had insisted. "No boring stuff!"

Mazie, who sat on the other side of the room, waved at Marylin to move her chair over so they could work together. But Mr. Holm made them count off like kindergartners, one-two, one-two, and Rhetta was one and Marylin was two, and that made them a pair.

Rhetta had turned around and looked Marylin straight in the eye. "I've got twenty-three interesting facts about me right off the top of my head. You ready to write?"

Marylin had nodded mutely. She pulled her

notebook and a pen out of her back pouch. She noticed that Rhetta's fingernails were alternately painted sparkly black and silver. It was actually sort of cool-looking, although not really Marylin's style.

"Fact number one: I am a Gemini," Rhetta reported. "Sign of the twins. Which is important, because I have a twin, only I don't know where."

"Were you adopted?" Marylin asked. She hadn't meant to get involved in an actual conversation with Rhetta, but she'd heard stories about twins separated at birth, how one twin would break his arm and the other would feel the pain all the way on the other side of the country. She'd always secretly wished for a twin, although one who lived with her, with whom she could communicate telepathically and also trade clothes.

Rhetta shook her head. "No, I mean like a soul twin."

"A soul twin?"

"Yeah, someone who's just like me, who really gets me, you know? I haven't met my soul twin yet, but I will one day. They're for sure an artist like I am. Do you like graphic novels?"

Marylin wasn't sure what a graphic novel was, so she shrugged. "I don't know."

And then Rhetta did something that surprised Marylin. She put her hand on Marylin's wrist, her silver and black fingernails sparkling like a handful of diamonds. "I think you'll like them if you give them a try. You're not like those other cheerleaders, I can tell."

"How do you even know I'm a cheerleader?"

Rhetta grinned. What was surprising was that she had a very friendly grin, and two dimples that Marylin was automatically envious of. When she smiled you could see how Rhetta Mayes must have looked when she was a little girl, before a veil of black hair and clothing had descended over her life. She had been cute, Marylin could tell.

"I saw you sitting with those girls at lunch, and I knew you were the cheerleaders. You can always tell. So's she"—Rhetta nodded toward Mazie—"but she's got a really cruddy aura, if you want to know the truth."

Then she reached her hand into her big black bag and pulled out a sketchbook. "This is the second amazing fact about me," she said, handing the book to Marylin. "I'm doing a graphic novel. I plan on publishing it when I'm finished."

Marylin opened the sketchbook. Inside, she discovered, was a world of fairies, some of them beautiful, others with squinched-up, mean faces, all of them looking so alive, Marylin was surprised they didn't fly off the pages. There were airborne fairies and fairies perched in trees, fairies having conversations with each other, and fairies dancing in circles around flowering bushes. The pages were laid out like a comic book, and the fairies spoke in balloons, except that there weren't any words yet.

"I'm not great at writing," Rhetta admitted. "I've got an idea for a story, but when I try writing it down in a script, it sounds dumb. Not like people—or fairies, really—would talk at all."

Then she leaned toward Marylin again. "You want to do it? I bet you can write, can't you? I can tell by looking at you that you have a way with words."

Marylin sat back in her seat. How did Rhetta Mayes know this about her? She couldn't, of course. They'd never seen each other in their lives before today. Rhetta couldn't know that Marylin had a journal she wrote in every night, or that she wrote poems that she never showed anyone, and at night she told stories to herself while she was waiting to fall asleep. Sometimes they were simple stories about having a nice boyfriend and going to dances. Other times her stories were more dramatic. Over the summer she had spent weeks working out a story where she saved a little girl who had been kidnapped by a wicked stepmother. In her story, there'd been a trail of clues she'd followed to where the little girl was hidden, and after she'd rescued the girl, she'd been invited to the White House to meet the president.

And some nights Marylin liked to imagine magical things as she drifted off to sleep. Kings and queens and dragons, good witches and bad witches, fairies and monsters. Paging through Rhetta's book, she saw pictures that could have been in the stories in her head, and a sudden constellation of ideas burst over her. What if the young fairy at the beginning of Rhetta's book got lost in the woods and the evil queen fairy, who ruled over all the others, refused to let them search for her because the evil queen fairy knew that the lost fairy was destined to take her throne upon being found? Marylin's fingertips tingled, and she grabbed her pen, ready to write.

But she made the mistake of looking at Rhetta. The spell was broken. She couldn't write a book with this strange girl and her jet-black hair and sparkly black and silver fingernails. How would she explain it to everyone? The very idea of writing a book with Rhetta Mayes didn't fit in with the ideas Marylin had about seventh grade and being a middle-school cheerleader and becoming best friends with Ruby Santiago, who, nice as she was, would definitely think Rhetta was weird and someone Marylin shouldn't be friends with.

"I wish I had time," Marylin said in her best middle-school cheerleader voice, handing the book back to Rhetta. "But with cheerleading and homework and everything, it's like I've got every minute of my day prescheduled."

Rhetta took the book and put it back in her black satchel, her eyes boring into Marylin the whole time. "I don't think 'prescheduled' is a word," she said icily. "Or if it is, it shouldn't be."

She turned her desk to face the front again. Marylin leaned forward and tapped her on the shoulder. "We have to do a report, remember? I haven't told you any interesting facts about me yet, and I need at least one more interesting fact about you."

Rhetta didn't say a word. She didn't even bother turning around.

Marylin sighed. She opened her notebook and began to write. *Rhetta Mayes is new to our school. She wishes she had a twin who liked art as much as she did. She is a good artist and one day hopes to write books called graphic novels. She has interesting fingernail polish.*

Then Marylin closed her notebook and put it back in her back pouch. She looked out the window at the woods that stood at the far edge of the soccer field. There, for just a second, she thought she saw a twinkling of light. Then it was gone.

Excitement tingled at the tips of Marylin's fingers again. The words of a story were gathering in her imagination. All she had to do was write them down. If she closed her eyes, she could see that lost fairy flying, hovering at the edge of the woods, looking for signs that would help her find her way back home. All Marylin had to do was grab her notebook out of her back pouch. All she had to do was write.

Marylin shook her head as though she were trying to shoo the very idea of fairies out of it. She had cheerleading practice and homework and chores to do. She didn't have time for writing stories.

"Come on, Marylin, I'll walk you to your locker."

Mazie stood beside her desk. The clock's

second hand ticked forward and the bell rang. Marylin stood up, picked up her back pouch, and followed Mazie out the door and into the hallway, where the lights flickered and burned, but did not sparkle, not even for a second.

dallas goes to the moon

Kate's first song was about rain falling softly against the windows on a summer night, but it was so dumb, she crumpled up the paper and threw it away. Her second song was about dogs. It was okay, but it didn't really fit with the idea of what kind of girl guitar player she wanted to be. She didn't want to be the kind of girl guitar player who wore gauzy skirts and had a dreamy expression on her face, and she didn't want to be the kind of girl guitar player who sang about pick-up trucks and how she wished she lived in the country, where everything was simple like in the good old days.

The more she thought about it, she realized

she wanted to be the kind of girl guitar player who wrote songs about a boy named Dallas. She did not personally know a boy named Dallas, but she could imagine a boy named Dallas, a boy with sandy brown hair falling over his blue eyes, a boy who thought girls who played guitar were the only girls worth knowing.

Kate's first song about Dallas was about how lonely Dallas got sometimes, even when he was hanging out with a bunch of his friends. She wrote about Dallas walking his dog down his street on an autumn day and seeing the last leaf fall from the oak tree on the corner. He looked at the leaf, then looked up at the window of a nearby house, where he saw a girl reading *The Giver*, which Kate just happened to be reading for language arts. At the end of the song, Dallas walked his dog back home, wondering if the girl in the window was as lonely as he was.

Kate started writing songs about Dallas on the first Saturday afternoon of October. By the following Saturday, she had written five Dallas songs. There was "Just a Boy Named Dallas," "Blue Skies Over Dallas's House," "The Girl in the Window," "I Wonder How Dallas Is Today," and a sad song called "Dallas Goes to the Moon," about Dallas falling in love with a girl who doesn't love him back. The girl's name was Alice, which was the only girl's name Kate could think of that rhymed with Dallas.

Flannery thought all the songs were too slow. "The words are good," she admitted, "and the music isn't bad, except that it sounds like you're playing at somebody's funeral."

Maybe it hadn't been such a great idea to go over to Flannery's house to get songwriting advice, Kate thought. In Kate's imagination, Flannery was like a slightly older sister, a little wiser, a little more experienced in the ways of the world. In real life, hanging out in her room, Flannery seemed more like an older sister who found you pretty irritating, but could put up with you for short periods of time when she was in the right mood.

Flannery leaned across the bed and took the

guitar from Kate. "Close the door, would you? My stepdad gets all hyper when I rock out." After Kate shut the door, Flannery turned up the amp and slid her fingers up and down the neck of the guitar, turning "I Wonder How Dallas Is Today" from a ballad into a punk rock song.

When she was finished, Kate took the guitar back from Flannery and played the song the way she had written it. "I just think it sounds better slow," she said when she was finished. "How you played it was good, but it doesn't sound like the song I was trying to write."

Flannery leaned back and propped her head against a giant teddy bear. "Who is this Dallas guy anyway?"

Kate shrugged. "Just somebody I made up. He's like a character in a story."

"Why don't you write about yourself instead of your imaginary friends?" Flannery asked, only sounding halfway sarcastic.

"What would I write about?" Kate strummed an F chord, the hardest chord there was. She spent thirty minutes a day practicing the F chord, and it still didn't sound right. "I'm not very interesting."

Flannery sat up. "Maybe. But you're more interesting than you look. I've always said that about you. Have you ever thought about bleaching your hair?"

Kate tried another F. "No, because I'm not insane." She glanced at Flannery's hot pink hair. "No offense or anything."

"None taken. But you know what your real problem is right now?"

"I didn't know I had a real problem," Kate said, even though it wasn't true. She could name at least four real problems she had at that very minute, including a three-page paper she had to write about the causes of the Civil War and a pre-algebra test on Tuesday.

Flannery stood up. She walked over to her dresser and leaned in closer to her mirror, like she was trying to get a better look at herself. Then she turned around and faced Kate. "Your real problem is that you're in love with this Dallas guy, and he's not even alive. You need somebody who's actually alive to be in love with."

She turned back to the mirror and combed her fingers through her hair. "Not that I believe that love exists or anything."

"One, I am not in love with a make-believe character," Kate insisted. She strummed the guitar hard, to underline her point. "And two, even though I believe love exists, I do not need to be in love with anyone. All I need to do is write songs and get at least a B-minus on my pre-algebra test. Preferably a B."

"Well, if you ever need some advice about how to get a real boyfriend, as in a boyfriend who's actually alive, let me know," Flannery said, applying mascara to her eyelashes. "I have lots of good tricks."

Kate did not want tricks for getting boyfriends. She just wanted to write songs about Dallas. She knew Dallas wasn't real, but she believed a boy like Dallas was out there somewhere, and she wanted to be ready for him when he showed up. *Listen to this song I just wrote*, she'd say, and he'd grin a wide, happy grin, because he'd finally found a girl who could play guitar and write songs. He'd finally found the girl he'd been looking for.

Sometimes at school Kate would look around for other seventh-grade girls who might be guitar players. She couldn't be the only one, could she? She couldn't be the only girl whose fingertips were so callused from holding down the strings that she could tap against them with her fingernail and hear a little click.

She was pretty sure she was the only girl wearing big, black lace-up boots, because so far most of the girls she'd seen wore tennis shoes, mostly white or grayish white, depending on how old the shoes were, with either pink or blue stripes. Really, she was a little surprised by how boring most people's shoes were. In Kate's opinion, what shoes you wore said a lot about your personality.

"Have you ever thought about ballet slippers?" Marylin asked her on the bus Monday morning. Even though they didn't walk together to the bus stop anymore, Kate and Marylin almost always sat with each other. It was nice, Kate thought, sort of like a family reunion with relatives you didn't see any other time of year. "I mean, I really like your boots, they make a total fashion statement and everything, but think about how light ballet slippers would feel on your feet."

Kate knew that Marylin was lying about liking her boots. She had seen Marylin looking at her boots with a definite "keep those things away from me" expression on her face. Still, she had to admire Marylin's restraint. It showed a certain maturity. In sixth grade, Marylin would have told Kate straight out how horrible she thought her boots were. Now she was trying to manipulate her. It was a big improvement, in Kate's opinion.

"I am not a ballet slippers kind of girl," Kate told Marylin. "I'm pretty sure you know that about me."

The weird thing was, sometimes Kate found herself wishing she *were* a ballet slippers kind of girl. She thought it might make life easier. Unfortunately, every time she tried to be that kind of girl, she felt like an entirely different person from who she actually was. She'd put on a dress and automatically feel like she should talk in a supersweet voice and never think mean thoughts and take baths instead of showers.

"Okay, so maybe ballet slippers aren't right for you," Marylin finally admitted as the bus pulled into the school driveway. "But I bet we could find some really cute shoes for you. I mean, cute shoes that are just your style. They could even be black, if you wanted."

"I have black shoes already," Kate said, pointing at her boots. "And they're the right shoes for me. Maybe you should think about getting some boots. They could change your life."

Marylin laughed, but Kate was serious. She worried about Marylin. When she bothered to look over at the middle-school cheerleaders' lunch table, Marylin seemed like a tiny mouse surrounded by hungry red-tailed hawks who were about to eat her alive in one tasty gulp. Sometimes Kate wanted to stomp over to the table, the thunk of her boots ringing through the cafeteria, and say, *Marylin is better than all of you added together, even if she cares too much about her hair.* Then she would sock Mazie Calloway in the nose and say, *You're not such a big deal. You're not even pretty.*

But as a rule, Kate was not the sort of person who socked people in the nose. So she sat at her usual table with Marcie Grossman, Amber Colbaugh, Timma Phipps, and Brittany Lamb, the same people she'd been eating lunch with since third grade, and didn't say or do anything except eat her sandwich, look at people's shoes, and make up song lyrics. Every once in a while she'd look toward the door, just in case a boy with sandy brown hair and blue eyes walked in and needed someone to sit with.

At lunch on Monday, just as Kate was finishing up her turkey and cheese sandwich and trying to come up with a word that rhymed with "aqua," Marcie Grossman asked her if she was staying after school that day. "It's Club Day, you knew that, right?" Marcie said, pulling some papers out of her backpack. "I've got the list right here of all the clubs seventh graders are eligible to join."

Kate had spent the weekend practicing guitar and looking up important Civil War facts on the Internet. She'd never gotten around to pulling out all the papers she'd collected from the previous week and stuffed in her binder—announcements for yearbook pictures and Pep Squad tryouts, forms for people interested in participating in the gift wrap and Read-a-Thon fund-raisers, the most recent updates to the student handbook. She supposed there was something in there about Club Day she'd never gotten around to reading either.

"Library Gang, Yearbook, Newspaper, Helping Hands Service Group, Hobby Club," Marcie read off the list. "Madrigal Singers (audition only), Jazz Band (audition only), Drama Club, Art Club, Cooking Club, Creative Writing Club, Whiz Kids Club, and then there's a bunch of boring stuff like Auto Repair. Why would anybody who didn't have a driver's license want to learn auto repair?"

"To get prepared for the future," Brittany

said. "Or if they wanted to steal someone's car. You know, they could figure out the wiring and everything."

Kate went over the list in her head. She knew her mom would let her pick only one thing, since Kate was the sort of person who liked to join clubs, but didn't actually like going to club meetings. She'd gotten kicked out of Girl Scouts in fifth grade because she missed seven meetings in a row. Kate had found that at the end of the school day, she preferred going home and reading rather than heading to the cafeteria, where the meetings were held every other week, the custodian mopping around everyone's feet as they made add-a-bead neck-laces and sit-upons. Her mom had gotten really mad at her when she'd gotten kicked out of Girl Scouts, since she'd spent a lot of money buying Kate a uniform and a handbook.

"I'm going to do Cooking Club," Timma said. "You get to make all this awesome stuff. Like fudge brownies and pumpkin pie and snickerdoodles."

"They ought to call it the 'Let's Get Fat'

Club," Marcie sneered. Marcie was always bragging about what a naturally thin person she was, but as Kate watched her scarf down five Oreo cookies, she had to wonder how long that would last.

"Let me see that paper," Kate said to Marcie, reaching her hand across the table. She scanned the list, mentally checking off the clubs she would never join, such as Madrigal Singers— she was an okay singer, but she hated wearing long dresses, which the Madrigal Singers had to do at their concerts—and Hobby Club, which she had heard was filled with boys who collected stamps and built replicas of Hogwarts out of toothpicks. Really, there were only two clubs Kate could imagine joining, Drama Club and the Creative Writing Club. Only she knew Drama Club was out of the question, because you did a lot of stuff on nights and weekends, and Kate's parents were totally against that.

Besides, Kate thought if she joined the Creative Writing Club, she might get feedback on her lyrics. Lyrics were a kind of poetry, right? Maybe there would be other songwriters in Creative Writing. Maybe they could start a singer/songwriter/guitar player club. At the high school where Kate's sister Tracie was a sophomore, they had a Friday night coffee-house, where people came and read poems and sang songs they'd written and played guitar. Acoustic guitar, Tracie had pointed out, not electric, but that was okay. Maybe Kate would switch over to acoustic guitar. Maybe the kids in the Creative Writing Club could start a Friday night coffeehouse at Brenner P. Dunn Middle School.

The girl who made the Creative Writing Club presentation after school at Club Day didn't strike Kate as the singer/songwriter/ guitar player type, but Kate thought she shouldn't judge people by appearances. This girl, who was wearing a denim jumper over a black turtleneck shirt and a pair of scuffed brown clogs, might be making a statement. She might be saying, *You don't have to be glamorous to be a writer, you just have to have a deep soul and a few black items in your wardrobe.* She could possibly have a guitar, Kate told herself as she signed up for the Creative Writing Club after the meeting, and shelves full of poetry books. Poets wore black all the time.

I bet she's got a pair of black boots in her closet almost exactly like mine, Kate thought as she walked toward the front of the school to catch the activities bus, but she's too shy to wear them. Kate told herself she could be a good influence on the denim jumper girl. *Don't be afraid to wear big boots*, she'd tell her after she'd gotten to know the girl a little bit. *Don't be afraid to be different. Different is better. Different is much more interesting.*

Different, Kate thought as she climbed on the bus, is everything.

Different, it turned out, could also be sort of irritating. "My name is Madison LaCarte," the denim jumper girl said at the first meeting of the Creative Writing Club, which took place on Thursday. "I'm related to Phyllis Petrie LaCarte, the famous author of historical novels, who is my great-aunt." Madison took a moment to look proud before adding, "I am following in her footsteps, of course. I have four hundred and twenty-nine pages of a novel set in medieval France. I would be happy to make copies for anyone who's interested, for the price of ten dollars, which covers all copying costs."

No one was interested, which did not surprise Kate one bit. You could tell just by looking at Madison LaCarte, who was once again wearing a jumper, this one made from tan corduroy material covered with red and yellow autumn leaves, that she was the kind of person who did tons of research and would include every fact she found in her book. You could also tell that her book would be incredibly boring, even if the writing was okay. Sadly, Kate was pretty sure now that Madison LaCarte did not have black boots or play guitar.

The other people in the Creative Writing Club had more potential. There were twelve of them besides Kate, ten girls and two boys. A few of the seventh-grade girls she knew from fifth and sixth grade, and one of the boys, Seamus Williams, had played on her coed soccer team in fourth grade. There was a girl dressed all in black Kate had never seen before, who introduced herself by saying she was new this year and was a terrible writer. A few girls giggled when she said that, and the new girl glared at them. "I bet you're all Ernest Hemingway," she sneered. "I bet you're all the greatest authors ever."

When it was Kate's turn to introduce herself, she said, "I've always liked writing. Mostly what I've written in my life is poetry, and now I'm writing a lot of song lyrics, since I also play guitar."

She looked around expectantly, waiting for the other songwriters and guitar players to announce themselves. But no one said anything. They just smiled at Kate like they thought what she said was nice, but not of particular interest to them personally. Kate held in a sigh, trying not to feel too disappointed. The girl next to her began introducing herself, saying her name was Lorna and she liked poetry too, especially the poems of Langston Hughes and Shel Silverstein.

That made Kate feel better because she also liked poems by Langston Hughes and Shel Silverstein. She looked at Lorna's shoes. Tennis shoes. New. White with a red stripe. Kate decided to take the red stripe as a sign that the girl was an original thinker.

During the next person's turn, Kate felt someone looking at her. She shifted her eyes left, then right, but couldn't catch anyone's eye. She sat very still. She could sense that who- ever was looking at her was sitting slightly behind her, but not all the way at the back of the room. Kate swiveled her head to the left and back, and that's when she caught him. He was an eighth grader who'd only said, "I like to write," when he introduced himself to the group and wouldn't elaborate when Ms. Vickery, their club adviser, had asked him to. "I just like to write, that's it," he'd said.

He'd said his name was Matthew Holler, and now he was staring at Kate. Kate thought about staring back, but she wasn't brave enough. Matthew Holler had hazel eyes and long, dark eyelashes and dark eyebrows, and he had to be almost six feet tall. He was beautiful, Kate realized suddenly as she stole another glance at him, although not everyone would notice this fact about him. Marylin, for instance, would notice his hair, which was too long to be respectable, even if it was wavy and a gold color that most girls would die for, and she'd notice his black T-shirt with a picture of the Ramones across the front. Kate did not know who the Ramones were, but they looked kind of weird and frightening. They looked like a band Flannery would like.

She didn't know why Matthew Holler was staring at her, and she wondered if he would say something to her when the Creative Writing Club meeting was over, but he didn't. He was the first person out of the room when Ms. Vickery said that was all for now, be sure to bring some writing to share for next week. He brushed past Kate's desk, and she smelled a clean, fresh smell, like he'd just taken his shirt out of the dryer. Kate watched Matthew Holler walk out of the room, his head bent forward, hands shoved in his pockets. She'd never had a boy stare at her that way before. She wondered if he played guitar.

At the next Creative Writing Club meeting, people read something they'd written, three poems or up to five pages of a short story. Madison LaCarte read five incredibly boring pages from her novel, and when Ms. Vickery asked if there were any comments, there was dead silence. Finally, when Kate thought the room might explode from everyone wanting to say how awful Madison's five pages had been, Matthew Holler raised his hand.

"The writing's pretty good, but it's all facts and no story," he said after Ms. Vickery called on him. "If I want to read history, I'll read a history book."

Kate sat back in her seat, stunned. She'd been thinking the same thing, only she hadn't been able to find the exact way to say it, unlike Matthew Holler, who'd nailed it right on the head. She turned to look at him, but he was doodling in his notebook. *Look at me*, Kate tried to ESP-message him, but he didn't.

"Well, I think you're very much mistaken," Madison told Matthew, her voice catching a little in her throat. Kate thought Madison might be about to cry, but it looked like that kind of crying that happened when you were so furious it was either cry or start screaming at the top of your lungs. "Anyway, what makes you so great? Let's hear what you wrote."

Madison crossed her arms over her chest and looked at the rest of the group, smirking. Matthew Holler shrugged and picked up his notebook.

"It's a haiku," he said. "That means—"

"A haiku is a form of poetry that originated in Japan," Madison jumped in. "Five syllables in the first line, seven in the second, five in the third."

"Why don't you let Matthew handle this, Madison?" Ms. Vickery said.

Madison harrumphed under her breath.

"Yeah, whatever, what she said," Matthew continued. "Anyway, this is called 'October Night':

"Cicada alone
Left to sing in the bare trees
Where did the sun go?"

It was not the poem Kate would have expected from a boy who looked like Matthew Holler. It was like a sad, sweet note played on a violin, held two seconds longer than the rest of the music. Kate wished she could raise her hand and say this, but she thought it would sound stupid when it came out of her mouth. Still, when she saw that Madison was about to say something, Kate jumped in, because she wasn't about to let Madison LaCarte, the most boring writer in the world, ruin the poem for everyone else.

"That's really beautiful," Kate said. Her face suddenly felt hot, but she forced herself to keep talking. "I mean, it's exactly the way the end of October makes you feel."

The girl next to her, Lorna, nodded. "I liked it a lot too," she said. Several other girls nodded and murmured, "Me too."

"Why does the cicada wonder where the sun

went when it's night?" Madison asked. "Isn't that kind of a stupid question?"

Kate looked at Matthew, who shrugged away Madison's remarks, like he wasn't interested in defending his poem. "It is what it is," he said.

"Nice work, Matthew," said Ms. Vickery, ignoring Madison's hand, which had popped up again and was wriggling wildly in Ms. Vickery's direction. "Now, who would like to read next?" She surveyed the room. "Kate?"

"Uh, I'm not sure I'm totally ready to read," Kate said, even though she had two new Dallas songs in her binder, freshly printed out on crisp, twenty-pound bond paper in Palatino Linotype font. She was about to say, "No, maybe next week," when she felt Matthew Holler looking at her. She turned to look at him, and he mouthed *Read* at her. *Yeah?* she mouthed back, and he nodded.

She looked at Ms. Vickery. "Uh, it's song lyrics," she explained. "I've been mostly writing songs, like I said last week." She cleared her throat and wished her hands weren't so shaky. "Uh, okay, I guess I'll start reading."

She read the lyrics to "A Little Bit of Something Sweet," a song about Dallas running into a girl he used to know back in fifth grade, only now she's fourteen, like Dallas, and the sort of girl like Kate would like to be, funny and smart-mouthed, nice underneath her tough exterior. She liked the chorus of the song a lot, which if she were singing the lyrics, she would have sung three times, once after each verse, but since she was speaking, she only read the chorus once:

"A little bit of something sweet
Underneath the saltiness
Tenderhearted beneath the calluses
A taste of something you can't forget."

Madison raised her hand. "You said 'something' twice. That's repetitive."

Kate looked down at her desktop. She noticed someone had written MEET ME AT THE END OF THE WORLD in red ink, and she wished she had time to think about this, what it might mean, who might have written it. Unfortunately, she was too busy feeling like the dumbest person on Earth. Whose stupid idea had it been to join Creative Writing Club, anyway? Why did she, Kate Faber, think she could write? Now, Matthew Holler, he was clearly a writer. Everybody recognized it immediately. Kate? She was just repetitive. And the word she'd repeated, "something," wasn't even an interesting word. It was a nothing word—

"Are you crazy?"

Kate looked up. Next to her, Lorna was glaring across the room at Madison LaCarte, her hands gripping the edge of her desk. "That was great!" Lorna exclaimed. "I can't believe someone our age wrote it. So what I'm trying to figure out is, why are you so critical of everyone? It's like you think you own this club, just because you were in it last year."

To Kate, it looked like Madison LaCarte actually crumpled, like a piece of tissue paper in the rain. Her shoulders slumped and her head drooped and the air seemed to go out of her entire body. When she looked back up, her face was flushed a deep red. "I'm sorry," she said in a subdued, but still sort of dramatic, voice. She paused a couple of seconds before saying, "And by the way, I know I use too many facts. I just hate to let any research go to waste." Then she looked at Kate. "And I actually thought your song was pretty good, even if I mostly listen to classical music."

"Thank you," Kate said. "I think once you put a little more story in your story, it will be good too. You write good sentences."

Madison LaCarte straightened up and beamed. "That's what my great-aunt Phyllis always says."

Next to her, Kate could hear Lorna stifling a giggle. Kate knew better than to look at her, or she'd start laughing too. A few seconds later Lorna nudged Kate with her elbow, and when Kate looked at her, Lorna rolled her eyes. Kate rolled her eyes back. And when she felt Matthew Holler looking at her, she turned straight around and grinned at him, a big, widemouthed grin.

Matthew Holler leaned his head back and smiled at the ceiling. Then he sat up again and looked at Kate. He looked at her without smiling, straight on and serious, until Kate had to look away. When the meeting was over, he left again without saying a word.

That night Kate tried to write a new song about Dallas, but she couldn't.

For some reason, Dallas didn't seem so real to her anymore.

The next day at lunch, Kate, Marcie, Timma, Amber, and Brittany were joined by Keith Lawton, an eighth grader who managed the girls' volleyball team and who could usually be found around groups of seventh-grade girls. Each day he chose a new table of girls to sit with and handed out advice to his lucky audience, who were usually thrilled to have an eighth-grade boy's attention. Kate personally didn't trust Keith Lawton. She suspected he'd been rejected socially by people his own age.

"Ladies! Ladies! Don't everyone fight over me! There's plenty to go around!" Keith said, scooching in next to Amber, a sack lunch in one hand, a book bag that looked like it weighed fifty pounds in the other. "Anyone want to share their fries?"

After Keith sat down, the conversation turned to the latest school scandal. Two days before, during C lunch, a group of vegetarians had staged a protest, bursting into the cafeteria with their faces covered in ketchup, yelling, "Meat is murder! Meat is murder!" at the top of their lungs. Apparently they wanted the cafeteria to stop serving hamburgers, although that information wasn't revealed until the next day, when there was a mediation meeting in the principal's office.

Kate listened, half-interested, tearing the crusts of her cheese sandwich into little pieces. Keith was saying that if you wanted to make changes, you should go through the appropriate government channels, and that the vegetarians should run for Student Government instead of interrupting everyone's lunch.

"I'm going to run for a seventh-grade representative seat," Marcie announced, which was news to Kate. "I think there are a lot of changes that need to be made at this school." She looked expectantly at Keith, waiting for him to approve of her decision, but he was looking off in the distance and not paying attention to Marcie's political ambitions.

"Oh God, look who it is." Keith pointed down the aisle between cafeteria tables. He rolled his eyes. "Kelly Fisherman. Why her parents don't send her to some kind of clinic is beyond me."

Kelly Fisherman weighed around two hundred pounds and had weird skin growths on her neck and face. In Kate's opinion, her personality was even more of a shambles than Madison LaCarte's. Kate thought that even if Kelly Fisherman were thin as a rail, she would probably not be a very popular person. She had a terrible temper and actually yelled at people when they made her mad, which Kate had seen her do just the week before, after a girl had missed a really easy basket in PE.

Nobody liked Kelly Fisherman, including Kate, and Kate felt bad about this. She was uncomfortable disliking anyone, having been disliked herself, but Kelly made it very hard for you to like her or even feel fondly toward her. All that was left for Kate to feel for Kelly Fisherman was sorry.

This was especially true two seconds later, when someone stuck a foot out and Kelly Fisherman went flying. The cafeteria was suddenly a volcano of laughter and hoots erupting everywhere. Keith Lawton was one of those silent laughers, Kate noticed. His mouth was open and his head was moving up and down, but no sound came out of him. Nevertheless, it was clear that he was very much enjoying the spectacle of Kelly Fisherman lying splat in the middle of the aisle, the contents of her tray rolling everywhere.

In the middle of the pointing and the hooting, Kate noticed a tall boy standing at a table a few rows away from the commotion, his palms flat down on the tabletop so that he was leaning over it, talking intensely to a scrawny kid with white blond hair and pimply skin. With a shock, she realized it was Matthew Holler. She'd never seen him in B lunch before. For a few seconds the commotion didn't seem to touch him, but finally he turned his head toward Kelly, who was still on the floor, too stunned to move.

Matthew Holler studied the sprawling figure of Kelly Fisherman on the cafeteria floor for a moment before turning back to his friend and flashing him the peace sign. Then he walked toward the lunch line, circling around Kelly, who was slowly rising to her feet and dusting herself off.

Kate watched as Kelly picked up her chips and her plastic-wrapped cookies, but abandoned her hamburger, which had flown off her tray and landed underneath a table. She seemed to be pretending that her two milk cartons, now leaking in the middle of the aisle, had nothing to do with her whatsoever.

After collecting her tray, Kelly Fisherman sat down at an empty table and began eating. Kate picked up her own sandwich, but was too distracted to eat it. Was Matthew Holler in B lunch? How could she not have noticed that before? She was searching her brain like crazy to think of other times she might have seen

Matthew in the cafeteria when she saw him returning from the lunch line, walking down the aisle like he wasn't thinking about anything in particular, just heading off somewhere after lunch. But as he passed Kelly Fisherman's table, he dropped two plastic-wrapped sandwiches on her tray. Kelly gave him a puzzled look and muttered a barely audible "Thank you," but Matthew was already halfway out the cafeteria door before the words left her mouth.

Kate was wondering if she was the only one who'd witnessed this amazing act when Keith Lawson said, "He is so weird."

"Who's so weird?" Marcie asked eagerly, turning her head left and right, looking for potential weirdos.

"Matthew Holler," Keith answered, as though it were obvious. "He lives on the next street over from me and we used to play together when we were kids, but now? Forget it."

"What was he like?" Kate asked, eager now herself for information. "I mean, when he was a kid?"

Keith gave her a strange look. "He was like a kid. Why do you want to know?"

Kate shrugged. "He just seems sort of cool."

"He gets in trouble all the time," Keith told her. "He used to be gifted, but now he just does regular classes. All he cares about is music."

That's when Kate knew that somewhere in his closet, Matthew Holler had a pair of boots that made his mother sigh and roll her eyes whenever he put them on. In fact, at that very moment, Kate felt like she knew everything worth knowing about Matthew Holler. She knew he thought different was good. She knew his fingers were calloused from hours of playing guitar, pressing down hard on the bottom two strings at the first fret with the tip of his index finger, doing it forever just to get the F to sound right. She knew so much about Matthew Holler that it didn't surprise her one bit when he came back into the cafeteria and walked up to her table.

"I want you to hear something," he said. "You got a minute?"

Kate nodded and stood up, abandoning her

lunch. She ignored the murmur of questions coming from Marcie, Amber, Brittany, and Timma. She ignored Keith Lawton's snort of disgust. When Matthew reached out his hand to her, she took it. She held it like a present. She tapped her fingertips against his fingertips and knew what she had always known, from the very first time she'd set eyes on him.

girl, dreaming

"You *have* to do this."

Mazie shoved a fluorescent yellow sheet of paper in Marylin's face. STUDENT GOVERNMENT ELECTIONS! the headline practically shouted at Marylin. BE A MOVER AND A SHAKER! MAKE DECISIONS THAT MATTER! REPRESENT YOUR CLASS!

"Why do I have to do this?" Marylin sat up from a hamstring stretch and tried to lean back out of Mazie's range. The way Mazie was waving that sheet around, someone was going to get a paper cut.

"Because we need representation!" Mazie threw her hands in the air like a politician making a speech, her voice bouncing over the gym's hardwood floors. "Our cheerleading uniforms are a joke. We look like kindergarten cheerleaders. And we need our own van for away games. And money so we can enter competitions."

"But what does that have to do with me?" Marylin asked, lying back on the mat and pulling one knee up to her chest. "Or with Student Government, for that matter?"

Mazie held up a finger. "One, Student Government makes recommendations to the school administration and the PTA about how much money should be spent every year on clubs. Cheerleading, for your information, is a club." She held up a second finger. "Two, you're our best candidate. None of the eighth-grade cheerleaders wants to run for Student Government because they're practically in high school and couldn't care less anymore. So that leaves you."

Marylin felt confused. There were five seventh-grade cheerleaders. Why her? Although, even as she thought this, a little flower of excitement bloomed inside her. Marylin McIntosh, Student

Government representative. It had a nice ring to it, she had to admit.

"I've got it all worked out," Mazie continued, taking a seat on the mat next to Marylin. "Ruby would really be the best person to run, but she's only allowed one extracurricular activity at a time. You're second prettiest after Ruby, plus you get good grades except in math. You didn't used to be popular, so the unpopular kids can relate to you. You're perfect for the job."

Marylin took the sheet of paper from Mazie and put it beside her on the floor.

"Let me think about it, okay?" she said. "Some of my classes are really hard this year."

"What's to think about?" Mazie asked, leaning forward in a long stretch. "There's nothing to it. You just show up at the meetings and vote the right way."

"Maybe," said Marylin. She stood up and stretched her arms toward the ceiling. She couldn't believe how sore her arms were after the routine they'd performed at Saturday's game, the one where she had to stand on her hands forever and then flip over into a bridge. "But I should still probably talk to my mom about it."

Actually, Marylin knew her mom would be thrilled if she ran for Student Government. Student Government was something that good kids did, kids who were already thinking about college in the seventh grade, kids who spent their weekends with their church youth groups building houses for homeless people. Clarissa Sharp, who was running for an eighth-grade representative seat, was always coming in during Marylin's art class to ask Mrs. Sage if she could stay after school to work on posters about ending world hunger and saving the environment.

Sometimes Marylin wanted to ask Clarissa if she could help her with her posters. Only she had cheerleading practice after school Monday through Thursday, and on Saturdays there was always one game or another to cheer for. In general, Marylin didn't have a lot of time for saving the world. But when she passed the art room on her way to the gym after the last bell and saw Clarissa bent over a piece of poster board, she got this excited feeling inside of her. She almost envied Clarissa Sharp for having such important work to do. She had to remind herself that Clarissa Sharp wasn't even pretty, and probably none of the eighth-grade football players even knew who she was.

"Well, ask your mom tonight," Mazie told Marylin as they walked to the other side of the gym, where the rest of the middle-school cheerleaders had gathered to start practice. "Because you should really start campaigning right away."

Then she smiled her best middle-school cheerleader smile. "Don't worry. With my help, you'll win by a landslide. I'll be your campaign manager."

Marylin had been afraid of that.

That night, Marylin called Kate. Kate was the one person she knew she could get the straight scoop from.

"You know, I think this is the first time you've called me since school started," Kate said the second she got on the phone. "Remember how in third grade we took turns calling each other to say good night?"

Marylin wished Kate wouldn't bring up the past. In fact, she wished that Kate wouldn't mention anything that made Marylin feel guilty or like a bad friend. Sometimes she felt like Kate was never going to let her forget that Marylin and Flannery had given her the silent treatment for weeks last year. Most people Marylin knew would have let it go by now. They would have let bygones be bygones. But not Kate. She liked things to be out on the table.

Personally, Marylin preferred things to be kept in drawers. Life was a lot neater that way.

"I'm thinking about running for Student Government," Marylin said, cutting off any discussion of how things had been in the old days. "But I wanted to get your opinion first. Good idea or bad idea? And if I did run, do you think I'd win?"

Kate was quiet for a moment. Marylin tried not to take this as a bad sign.

"Last question first: Yes, I think you'd win,"

Kate said finally. "You're popular, but people don't hate you. Not yet, anyway. Is it a good idea? I don't know. I guess it depends on why you want to do it."

"To make a difference," Marylin said, only it came out sounding more like a question.

"That's pretty unspecific, don't you think? What kind of difference do you want to make? Who do you want to make a difference for?"

Now it was Marylin's turn to be quiet. She couldn't say she wanted to make a difference for middle-school cheerleaders. No one would vote for her. Besides, she realized, she didn't care about making a difference for middle-school cheerleaders. She thought their uniforms were cute. She had fun riding to away games on the team bus.

On the other hand, she realized suddenly, she would like it if the fruit they served in the cafeteria didn't have brown spots on it. The apples were always mealy and mushy, and the bananas looked like they were five minutes away from turning completely black. She would like it if Walt Sevier, who had muscular dystrophy and had to walk with crutches, could get through the hallway in the morning without always getting pushed to the wall. She would like it if the janitor, Mrs. Mosely, had a real office and not just an oversize closet with a student desk in it.

"Does that sound right?" Marylin asked after she'd told Kate her thoughts. "Or is it stupid?"

Kate laughed. "That's the least stupid thing you've said in over a year. No offense or anything. My only advice would be, come up with two things that everyone would think were really cool, like having a movie afternoon one Friday a month, where they'd cancel classes and show a video in the auditorium instead."

"But that could never happen," Marylin pointed out.

"Of course it could never happen," Kate replied. "The point is, it makes people think you're looking out for their needs. So they elect you, and then you take care of Mrs. Mosely."

"Isn't that like lying?"

Kate took a second to answer. "Think of it more like dreaming out loud," she said. "The fact is, if you could get a movie afternoon for everyone once a month, you'd do it, right?"

"Sure," said Marylin. "I love that idea."

"So it's not a lie," Kate concluded. "It's a kind of wish that you're sharing with other people."

Before she could stop herself, Marylin blurted out, "Would you help with my campaign? I mean, come up with ideas and stuff?"

"Like be your campaign manager?"

Marylin automatically regretted saying anything. Mazie was supposed to be her campaign manager. But Marylin knew that Kate would do a million times better job. Kate could get her elected.

And just like that, Marylin knew getting elected to Student Government was what she wanted more than anything else in the world.

"Sure," Marylin said. "You could be my manager. I mean, Mazie sort of said she'd do it, but you probably have more time than she does and everything."

"You mean I'd actually do a good job," Kate corrected her.

"You'd do a great job," Marylin agreed.

"Mazie's going to be mad if you tell her I'm doing it instead of her."

"Mazie's always mad about something," Marylin said, which made her giggle.

Kate giggled too. "Mazie's a jerk."

Marylin felt like she should stick up for Mazie, even though she was pretty sure Mazie would never stick up for her. "But she *is* my friend."

"Well, your friend's a jerk," Kate replied, still giggling.

Marylin couldn't help herself. She started to laugh uncontrollably. "I know!" she shrieked. "I know!"

Later, after she'd hung up the phone, Marylin felt light and airy, as though she'd just shrugged off a backpack filled with bricks and could finally stand up straight and breathe. She knew she would be in big trouble with Mazie, but for some reason she didn't care. She was going to run for Student Government and win. She was going to save the world, or at the very least get better bananas in the cafeteria.

✳ ✳ ✳ ✳ ✳

On Saturday, after cheering at the football game, Marylin and her little brother Petey went to their dad's apartment, where they were going to spend Saturday and Sunday night. On Monday morning, Mr. McIntosh would drive them to school. Marylin hated this routine, which they went through twice a month. She didn't hate seeing her dad, she just hated having to switch around her life. She felt like her parents ought to be the ones who switched their lives around, since they were the ones who had gotten a divorce and ruined everything.

The worst part, in Marylin's opinion, was the drop-off. Marylin's parents not only no longer loved each other, they didn't seem to like each other very much. They pretended that they did, but when they talked to each other it was like every word came with a little knife attached to it.

"Petey has to go to bed at a reasonable hour," her mom told her dad as she handed him Petey's suitcase through the apartment doorway. "I'd really, really appreciate it if just this once you could put Petey's real needs first. He doesn't need to watch movies until midnight. He needs to sleep."

"Petey always goes to bed by ten on Saturdays and nine thirty on Sundays," Marylin's dad said. He rubbed Petey's head. "Don't you, Pete-ster?"

"Seventy-four percent of the time," Petey replied.

"A hundred percent of the time would be preferable," Marylin's mom said.

"Yep, in a perfect world, it sure would be." Marylin could tell her dad was trying to sound agreeable, but it was hard to do that through clenched teeth.

"And please get the kids to school on time," Marylin's mom continued. "They're not in pre-school anymore, where it doesn't matter if they show up ten minutes late."

"That only happened once," said Mr. McIntosh. "And only because I had to stop for gas."

"Maybe you should fill up on Sunday," Marylin's mom—who used to be Mrs. McIntosh but was now Ms. Fuller—said. "Plan ahead."

"For a change?" Marylin's dad asked.

"I didn't say that."

"But you were thinking it."

"Could we go inside now?" Marylin asked, wanting more than anything in the world to get away from this conversation. "I have to start working on my Halloween costume."

Marylin had her own room in her dad's apartment. It was half the size of her room at home, but she didn't mind. It had a cozy feeling to it. Her dad had let her pick the furniture and put up whatever posters she wanted, and Marylin had been very careful about what she chose. She picked colors in the light bluish green family for the paint and the curtains. All the furniture was painted white. It was the country cottage look, which she knew from reading her mom's magazines. As long as Marylin didn't look out the window, she could pretend she lived in a cozy cottage somewhere in England, and any minute someone would come over for tea. Marylin didn't even like tea, but she liked the *idea* of having tea, especially if it was served in white cups with old-fashioned pictures of roses on them.

If Marylin made the mistake of looking out

the window, she saw a parking lot, and beyond that the back of a strip mall where a bunch of skateboarders were always hanging out. It completely ruined the country cottage feel of her room, so she tried never to look out the window.

It had taken her forever to find the right bedspread for her room. Nothing at the mall matched the pictures in her head. Finally, in August, when she'd gone with her dad and Petey to the flea market at the county fairgrounds, she'd found a quilt in a Star of David pattern, with green and blue and pink all through it. It had cost two hundred and fifty dollars, but ever since her parents had gotten divorced, Mr. McIntosh pretty much bought Marylin and Petey whatever they wanted, so he paid for the quilt without complaining about how expensive it was.

Now Marylin carefully spread out her clothes for the weekend on top of her bed, refolding them before putting them in her dresser. She always brought too many clothes. Not only did she have to pack for the weekend, she also had to pack for Monday morning. On Fridays, when she packed, she couldn't possibly predict what her mood would be on the following Monday, so she had to give herself options.

For this trip, Marylin had had to pack two suitcases, one with regular clothes and one with materials to make her Halloween costume. Halloween was Tuesday, and the middle-school cheerleaders had decided to come to school dressed for the occasion. Ruby was going to be a nurse, Ashley was going to be a hippie, and Mazie was going to be a bee. Marylin thought that going as a bee was a mistake, since a bee costume could only make you look round and lumpy, and nobody looked good in yellow tights. She hadn't said this to Mazie, of course. Mazie thought that going as a bee was the best idea ever invented on the planet, and Marylin wasn't going to be the person who told her otherwise.

Marylin was going as a fairy princess. She had considered all sorts of other ideas, a cell phone, a peanut butter and jelly sandwich, Sleeping Beauty, Pocahontas, but no matter how many ideas she came up with, she kept going back to being a fairy princess. First of all, fairy princesses were pretty, and Marylin liked being pretty. Second, she knew about fairy princesses. She had imagined them, dreamed about them, read book after book about them. She was practically a fairy princess expert.

And then there was the fact that for the last two months, ever since the beginning of school, she had been sneaking peeks at Rhetta Mayes's drawing journals. Really, all Rhetta Mayes did was draw, and pretty much all she drew were fairies. Rhetta never spoke to Marylin, but sometimes she seemed to sense that Marylin wanted to see her drawings, and she would hold her sketchbook out so Marylin could get a better look.

Marylin didn't just look at Rhetta's pictures; she stepped into them. On bad days, days when it was raining and Marylin's feet had gotten wet, or days when Mazie was in a bad mood and made critical comments about everyone in the world, including the other middle-school cheerleaders, expecting Marylin to agree 100 percent, Marylin looked forward to going to pre-algebra or language arts, classes she had with Rhetta, just so she could spend some time in one of Rhetta's pictures. Life was easier when you could escape it every once in a while.

She would have liked to have gotten Rhetta's advice on her fairy costume. As it was, Marylin had to settle for borrowing Rhetta's ideas. One of her fairies who showed up in almost every story really did look like a princess, with a crown of roses and a gauzy-looking skirt that fell around her legs like rose petals. This was the fairy princess Marylin wanted to be.

Taking the pink material her mother had helped her buy at Jo-Ann's out of her suitcase, she wished she'd started on her costume a week ago. But this year Marylin was discovering she didn't always have time to get ready a week ahead, not with homework, cheerleading practice, and dealing with her parents' divorce filling up her days. How were you supposed to get prepared for Halloween when you were always packing to go back and forth between your parents' houses? Besides being depressing, Marylin found her parents' breakup completely inconvenient.

Marylin took out her mother's sharp-bladed scissors, which Petey was under no circumstances allowed to get close to. She took out the pad of drawing paper she'd tried to copy Rhetta's fairies onto from memory. Then Marylin sat on her bed and wondered what in the world she was doing. She didn't know how to sew. She'd thought it would just come to her, but now she realized it wouldn't.

"Honey, do you want a snack?" Marylin's dad poked his head in the doorway. "I've got some pizza rolls in the freezer."

"No, I'd better get started on this," Marylin said, pointing to the yards of material on her bed. "You don't know anything about sewing, do you?"

Mr. McIntosh came in and sat next to Marylin on the bed. "As a matter of fact, I do," he told her. "In high school and college, I did a lot of theater, and we were always having to make our own costumes. I even know how to use a sewing machine, believe it or not."

"You do?" Marylin was stunned. In her entire life, she had never met anyone besides Kate's mom who knew how to use a sewing machine, and now it turned out her very own father could. She leaned back and looked at her dad for a long time. She wondered what else about himself he hadn't told her.

"Yep," he said. "Sad to say, I don't have a sewing machine on the premises. But I know how to use a needle and thread. Despite what your mom says, I'm a very handy guy."

Marylin picked up the edge of the pink fabric and rubbed it between her thumb and index finger. She hated it when her dad made comments like that. They weren't exactly critical of her mom, but at the same time they were. It made Marylin feel like she was in the middle of somebody else's fight and each person expected her to take sides. This was one of her least favorite feelings in the world.

"So will you help me make my costume?"

Marylin asked. "I can show you some pictures of what it's supposed to look like."

"How about I teach you how to sew? I'll help you help yourself."

Marylin giggled. "I thought moms were supposed to teach their daughters how to sew."

"Welcome to the twenty-first century, sweetheart," her dad said. "It's a brand-new ballgame."

"Can I help?" asked Petey, walking into the room and plopping into Marylin's rocking chair. "I'm pretty creative."

Marylin pulled a plastic bag from her suitcase and shook it out on the bed. Out tumbled a dozen artificial flowers and a length of middle-weight wire. "Can you make a crown of roses? One that wouldn't look stupid?"

Petey shrugged. "Why not? I built an entire nuclear reactor out of Legos once. A crown of roses ought to be a snap compared to that."

"Let's get started then," Mr. McIntosh said, standing. "We'll spread this fabric out on the dining-room table and cut out the pieces."

Marylin followed her dad and Petey out of

her room. She carried the scissors, her sketch-book, a spool of pink thread, and a yard of elastic for the rose petal skirt's waistband. It occurred to her that it was sort of funny that she was getting help on her fairy princess costume from her dad and her little brother. It made her wish Kate was there. Kate was the sort of person who could appreciate how weird life could get sometimes, probably because she was so weird herself.

But weird in a good way, Marylin thought as she walked into the dining room. And, to her surprise, she realized she meant it.

Kate was waiting for her at the front of the school Monday morning with a pile of posters that she'd made over the weekend. "I hope you like these, because I made about fifty of them," she said, handing one to Marylin the second she saw her. "My dad actually let me use his color printer, which is an amazing event. He says if he could, he'd vote for you."

Marylin examined the poster. Kate had used Marylin's sixth-grade school picture, the one that made her look like she was at least in ninth grade, so that was good. She had had a streak of bad school picture luck from second through fifth grade, closed eyes, stupid expressions, and one really bad hair day. Her mom had gotten in the habit of ordering the smallest picture package over the years, just because she always ended up putting Marylin's school pictures in the bottom of her desk drawer, they were that bad.

But her sixth-grade picture made her look mature and pretty, someone you would vote for to represent you, in Marylin's opinion. Below her picture on the poster were the words INTEGRITY. COMPASSION. NEW IDEAS. VOTE: MARYLIN MCINTOSH, SEVENTH-GRADE STUDENT GOVERNMENT REPRESENTATIVE.

"Wow, this is great, Kate," Marylin said. "I mean, it looks professional and everything."

"Well, my dad helped," said Kate, sounding pleased. "He's worked on some city council campaigns, so he's pretty good at this kind of stuff. But the main ideas were mine."

Marylin liked the posters so much, she

almost forgot to be nervous about seeing Mazie when she got to her locker. She hadn't told Mazie yet that Kate was going to be her campaign manager. As far as she knew, Mazie hadn't given a second thought to Marylin's campaign after she'd made sure that Marylin filled out the forms to officially become a candidate. So maybe she wouldn't be mad that Kate was doing all the hard work.

As it turned out, Mazie was not amused.

"You're kidding me, right?" she said after Marylin had shown her the posters before first period. "Kate Faber? I mean, I know you guys used to be friends, but she's so lame. Have you seen those boots she wears? And now she hangs around with Matthew Holler, who's, like, halfway to dropping out of school."

Matthew Holler? Marylin had no idea who Matthew Holler was. How could she not know about a boy in Kate's life? Wasn't that against the rules for one friend not to share important boy information with another friend? Marylin didn't know whether to feel mad or a little bit sad that Kate hadn't said a word to her about this Matthew Holler person.

"But you have to admit, it's a good poster," Marylin insisted. "Her dad runs all sorts of political campaigns, so it's really him who's doing it."

Mazie rolled her eyes. Just then, Ruby Santiago walked up. She took the poster Marylin was holding and looked at it. "Wow," she said after a moment. "This is awesome."

"Kate Faber made it for me," Marylin said quickly, hoping she might get some support for Kate from Ruby. "She's really talented."

"Hmm, I don't think I know her," said Ruby, handing the poster back to Marylin. "But she did a great job on this poster."

"How can you not know her?" Mazie asked, sounding irritated. "She was in our pod last year, in Mrs. Watson's homeroom."

Ruby shrugged. "Sorry."

Marylin was a little shocked that Ruby didn't know who Kate was, but she guessed if you were Ruby Santiago, you could afford to not know all sorts of people.

"Well, fine then," Mazie said to Marylin, shutting her locker door a little harder than necessary. "Let Kate do the hard work. While she's at it, tell her to write your speech for tomorrow, if she hasn't already."

"Tomorrow?" Marylin felt a bolt of panic fly through her. "I didn't know I had to give a speech tomorrow."

"Didn't you read the candidates' checklist?"

"What checklist?" Marylin ran over a mental list of everything in her back pouch and binder. She was a very organized person, and she couldn't remember a thing about a checklist.

Mazie put her hand over her mouth and giggled. "Whoops! I guess I forgot to give that to you. I picked it up when I got your candidate registration forms. It's in my locker somewhere. I'll give it to you at lunch."

"I can't believe you forgot to tell me I have to make a speech tomorrow!" Marylin was shaking with anger. How could Mazie forget something so important?

"Get over it, Marylin," Mazie said. She gave Marylin a backward wave as she turned right on C hallway and headed toward her first-period class. "It's just a stupid speech. It's not even important."

Marylin turned in the opposite direction. Of course the speech was important. It could make or break her campaign. And now, for the life of her, Marylin couldn't think of one thing to say. All she could think of was that tomorrow was Halloween and she had to give the speech of her life, and she was going to be dressed up as a fairy princess.

Everything's going to be fine, she tried to convince herself as she walked into art. But she knew it wouldn't be, not unless she could convince everyone in the seventh grade that voting for Tinkerbell was a great thing to do.

Which she was pretty sure she couldn't.

Mr. Faber was the one who came up with the opening line for Marylin's speech. He, Kate, and Marylin had been working on it since dinner, which they'd eaten while sitting around Mr. Faber's laptop at the kitchen table.

"How's this," he'd asked around nine thirty,

which was officially the time Marylin was supposed to be home. "I can't grant your wishes, but I can help with your dreams."

"That's close," said Kate, tapping her pencil against her forehead, like it might help her think. "But it's not quite there yet. How about something like, 'I can't make your wishes come true, but I can grant, um, something . . .'"

"But I can help make your dreams come true!" Mr. Faber exclaimed, typing rapidly on his laptop. "Excellent! 'I can't make your wishes come true, but I can help make your dreams come true.'" He looked over at Marylin. "What do you think, Mary-Lou?"

"I . . . like it," Marylin said haltingly. "Except it's sort of dramatic. Because, really, I can't make anybody's dreams come true."

"Sure you can," Mr. Faber insisted. "If we're talking about dreams for a better school, right?"

Marylin thought about this for a moment. Then she nodded. "I guess that's what I'm talking about," she said. "If that's not too dumb," she added.

"Not dumb at all!" said Mr. Faber, still typing. "Now all we have to do is incorporate your list of campaign points"—he paused to briefly lift up the sheet of paper Marylin had printed out earlier with bullet points of all her campaign promises—"and you'll have yourself a speech."

The next morning she got out of bed, brushed her teeth, and did her best not to throw up. Throwing up on any occasion would have been bad enough, but throwing up and ruining her fairy princess costume would have been a disaster. It would have been like throwing up on the *Mona Lisa*, in Marylin's opinion, because her fairy princess costume had turned out to be a work of art.

"Petey made that crown?" her mother asked at breakfast. She turned to Petey. "I had no idea you could do something like that."

"That's sort of an insult, if you think about it," Petey said through a mouthful of muffin. "But I won't take it personally."

"No, it's just . . . so beautiful," said Marylin's mom, sounding like she might cry. She reached over and touched Marylin's skirt. "You guys really made this with Dad?"

Marylin nodded. "He's really good at making costumes. You'd think I would have known that before, but I didn't."

"Well, your dad was always so busy, traveling all the time for work," Marylin's mom said. "He made you that frog costume when you were two. Do you remember that?"

"I remember seeing a picture of it," said Marylin. "I don't remember actually wearing it."

"Everybody loved that costume," Marylin's mom said. "It's too bad Dad didn't have more time later to do that kind of thing. I know he would have loved to."

Marylin thought it was strange to hear her mom talking about her dad and sounding sad instead of angry. Maybe this was the start of something. Maybe her mom would stop being angry, start being sad for a while, and then go all the way back to being in love with her dad again.

She leaned over and tapped her mom with her wand. "I can't make your wishes come true," she said. "But I can help make your dreams come true."

Marylin's mom gave her a funny look. "What's that supposed to mean?"

"I'm not sure in this situation," Marylin said. "But I'm glad you like my costume."

A lot of people, it turned out, liked Marylin's costume. When she walked up onstage to give her speech, a row of football players sitting in the back of the auditorium stomped their feet and whistled. "I'll vote for you!" one of them shouted out, and a chorus of "Me too!" echoed back. Teachers massed in the aisles and started shushing everyone like crazy.

Marylin found Kate in the middle row, where she'd promised to sit so Marylin could pretend she was just talking to a friend instead of doing something terrifying like giving a speech to two hundred seventh graders.

"I can't grant your wishes," Marylin began, and then headed into her speech. She talked about the cafeteria, she talked about helping out handicapped kids, she talked about pizza every day for lunch and movie afternoons once a month. "I promise I will do a good job," she ended up. "I will work hard for you and will represent your needs and concerns to the student government. I can't do it with a wave of my magic wand, but I can do it with your vote. Thank you very much."

The applause was loud and enthusiastic. Marylin saw Kate clapping with her hands extended up in the air. She saw Ruby Santiago clapping in a medium sort of way. She saw Mazie and Ashley whispering to each other. They weren't clapping at all.

And then she saw Rhetta Mayes, who wasn't clapping either. She was drawing. Marylin would have liked to know what Rhetta thought about her speech, and more importantly, what Rhetta thought about her costume. In fact, suddenly it seemed important for her to know. So when she left the stage, she didn't go sit with the other middle-school cheerleaders, she went and sat by Rhetta.

Rhetta ripped a page out of her sketchbook. "This is for you," she said, not actually looking at Marylin.

Marylin took the picture. It was her. It was Marylin McIntosh dressed as a fairy princess with a crown of roses on her head. In her hand, she held two campaign signs. One said, TO VOTE . . . and the other one said, . . . PERCHANCE TO DREAM.

"Could I use this?" Marylin asked. "I mean, for a campaign poster?"

Rhetta nodded. "Sure. If you want to."

"I do," said Marylin. She sat back in her seat. Another candidate, Calvin House, started his speech, but Marylin couldn't make herself pay attention. She kept looking at Rhetta's drawing. Maybe if Marylin were elected, she could make Rhetta the official Class Artist. There could be a Class Artist and a Class Poet, which would be Kate, and a Class . . . Well, Marylin had run out of ideas for the moment, but there might be lots of official class offices people could hold.

The election was a week away. There would be a debate between the candidates on Friday. There would be more handshaking, e-mailing, and campaigning in the cafeteria during lunchtime. There would be more promises. But for now there was the dreaming. Marylin leaned her head back against her seat and closed her eyes. She imagined an army of fairies fluttering through the school hallways, the air shimmering around them as they touched their wands to lockers and water fountains and classroom doors, making everything perfect with a wave of their tiny hands.

what do your words say?

When Kate was in fifth grade, she had bought a book called *How to Improve Your Vocabulary in Ten Minutes a Day*. Well, it had actually been a booklet, and her mom had bought it when Kate spotted it in the grocery store checkout line. Kate hadn't particularly cared about improving her vocabulary, she'd just wanted to buy something, and she knew her mom wasn't going to buy the Twix bar she'd initially had her eye on.

But reading the booklet on the way home from the store, Kate had gotten interested. She believed automatically what the author, Eugene K. Watsonberg, said—that words were important. "Words say something," Eugene K. Watsonberg had written. "What do your words say about you?"

At home, Kate had gotten out a brand-new notebook she'd been saving to start a new project in. Kate loved starting new projects, which is why she always kept notebooks handy. For her last project, she'd drawn an intricate map of her neighborhood, complete with trees, mailboxes, and yard art, and had spied on her neighbors and recorded information about them. Unfortunately, her neighbors didn't come out much, so that particular project had petered out after three days.

To be honest, most of Kate's projects fizzled after three days, which had been true (sort of) of her Improving Her Vocabulary project as well. Except that even after Kate had stopped picking a new word from the dictionary every morning to memorize and use at least five times during the day, she still kept noticing interesting words and kept a list in her head of her favorite and least favorite words. Her favorite words included *cashmere*, *blue*, *rodeo*, and *sizzle.* Her least favorite words were *pimple*, *mucus*, and *fink.*

Now that she was in seventh grade and turning into a songwriter and a poet, Kate thought she ought to write down her special words in a poetry notebook. She would carry the notebook in her backpack so she would always have her words with her. She got this idea on a Saturday morning, and she liked it so much, she immediately hopped out of bed and went looking for her mom, whom she found in the kitchen looking through a book of wedding cake recipes.

"Are you going to the store today?" Kate asked her, not even bothering to say "Good morning" first. "Because I need a new notebook. For school."

Mrs. Faber looked at Kate and raised an eyebrow. "Didn't I buy you ten new notebooks, each a bright neon hue, at the beginning of the school year, which was"—and here Mrs. Faber checked her watch—"a mere two and a half months ago?"

"It's December second, Mom," said Kate,

pointing to the calendar by the refrigerator, which she noticed was still on the November page. She walked over and flipped it to December. "So I've been in school three months. Time for a new notebook!"

Mrs. Faber squinted her eyes at Kate. "You're starting a new project, aren't you? I can tell by the look on your face. You can't fool me."

"At least I don't want horseback-riding lessons," Kate replied, smiling in what she hoped was a winning way. Kate's big dream in fourth grade had been to learn to ride a horse, but when her mother had finally signed her up for lessons, Kate discovered she was scared to death of horses. Unfortunately, Mrs. Faber had paid for the lessons in advance and the money was nonrefundable. It was Kate's most expensive project, and her mom had never let her forget it.

"True enough," Mrs. Faber said, standing up and stretching. "In comparison, a notebook is a cheap and easily attainable thing. And I'm going to the grocery store after lunch, so I can pick one up for you then."

Kate took a deep breath. She knew she was pushing it, but she had a vision for her notebook, and it didn't involve the $1.99 kind you got at Food Lion. "I was sort of hoping you might take me to Hobson's. I'll buy the notebook with my own money and everything. I just need you to drive me."

Hobson's was a store for people who liked paper and pens and rubber stamps and India ink. It was sort of like an art store and sort of like the fanciest Hallmark store in the world. Kate loved it. There were stacks of thick, creamy paper, which sold for twenty-five cents a sheet: dove white, pearl gray, lemon yellow, pale blue. There were fountain pens with nibs that Kate knew she was far too messy to use, but she liked the idea of. You could buy charcoal pencils and sketchbooks there, and brushes and watercolor kits. There were journals and diaries and notebooks, of course, with lined or unlined paper and thick cardboard covers—some plain and brown, others with famous paintings on them.

Kate wanted a notebook with lined pages,

college ruled, with a cardboard cover she could decorate herself. She also wanted a new pen, felt-tipped, fine line, black ink. No, blue ink. Indigo blue, a color she was sure she could only get at Hobson's. Just the other night on the phone, she and Matthew Holler had agreed that the right pen was very important when it came to writing poetry. Matthew, she'd learned, used any pen handy for doing homework, a pencil for math, and a Pilot Precise V5 when he was working on a poem.

Mrs. Faber poured herself a cup of coffee. "I'll take you to Hobson's on one condition," she said after a minute of thinking about it. "You tell me what the notebook is really for."

"Words," said Kate. "It's for writing down words."

"Could you be more specific?" Mrs. Faber asked. "You've just summed up the use of almost every notebook on the planet."

"What about notebooks for writing down numbers?" Kate asked.

Mrs. Faber sighed. "Okay, yes, you've got me there. Do you want to go to Hobson's or not?"

"It's for writing down good words," Kate said quickly, not wanting to irritate her mom any more than she already had. "Beautiful words. Like words you would use in a poem."

Now, Mrs. Faber liked poetry. She still had all her poetry books from her college English classes tucked away in the family-room bookshelf, including *The Collected Poems of William Carlos Williams, Volume I* and *Geography III* by Elizabeth Bishop, a book that Kate had read bits and pieces of and pretty much liked except for when it got boring.

"That's a good reason to get a new notebook," Mrs. Faber agreed. "Well, let me take a shower and try to look respectable. If we're going to Hobson's, I should at least put on some mascara."

"You don't need makeup, Mom," Kate said. "You are a natural beauty."

Mrs. Faber laughed, like she thought Kate was joking around. Actually, Kate wasn't, but you couldn't say something like that and sound all serious about it. People might get the wrong idea about you if you said that sort of thing in a serious tone of voice. They might figure out that you loved them.

It was like carrying a bird in her backpack—something light, with wings, and filled with bits and pieces of songs. All day on Monday, Kate was aware of her new notebook as she went from class to class. She practically expected it to fly out into the hallway and dart from locker to locker.

She wanted to show it to Matthew Holler, but she couldn't. Which, she thought, wasn't exactly fair, since in the time that she and Matthew Holler had been friends, he had shared all sorts of things with her.

The day Matthew had grabbed Kate's hand and pulled her out of the cafeteria, he had taken her to the school's audiovisual lab. Brenner P. Dunn Middle School was famous for its state-of-the-art technology. People moved twenty miles just so their children could go to Brenner P. Dunn Middle School and get their hands on its computers and digital recording equipment. Every time there was a school assembly, the principal went on and on about the fascinating and educational projects students were doing in the audiovisual lab. "We are the middle school of people's dreams," she liked to say.

Matthew Holler's fascinating and educational project involved a lot of noise at very loud levels. Guitar noise, drum noise, and some noise that sounded like a tractor running over half a dozen metal trash cans. "It's industrial," he explained to Kate, and Kate had nodded as though she halfway knew what he was talking about. She didn't, but she didn't care. All she cared about was that Matthew Holler wanted her to hear his music.

"It's really cool that you're into music and everything," he'd said to her as they listened to screeching brakes whining over a battalion of guitars. "I think you're the first girl I ever met who played guitar."

She almost said, "Flannery does too," but she stopped herself. She didn't know if Matthew Holler and Flannery knew each other, but it occurred to her that they might be each other's type. Kate suspected that if Matthew found her interesting, he'd find Flannery very interesting.

"I don't know many people at all who play guitar," Kate said. "I've sort of been hoping I'd meet some other guitar players one of these days."

That sounded stupid. That sounded so dumb Kate thought she might cry. But Matthew Holler just said, "Yeah, it makes a big difference in life when you find your tribe. I don't have one friend who's not completely obsessed with music."

Kate didn't know if she was completely obsessed with music or not. At home her parents mostly played the classical radio station, so when she was downstairs that's what she listened to. She had a boom box in her room, which she kept tuned to KISS 101.5, which claimed to play "the biggest hits to hit your eardrums," with commercial-free Mondays and Top-40 Tuesdays. But ever since she'd started playing guitar and writing songs, she found herself getting irritated with the songs on KISS 101.5. Most of the words were dumb, and it seemed like every song they played was either about falling in love or falling out of love or getting your heart broken.

"What radio station do you listen to?" she'd asked Matthew after they left the media lab and were walking down the hall to their fifth-period classes. "Because I wish there was a station that played something good all the time."

"I listen to K-DUCK," he told her. "It's a college station, 88.9. There's always something different on it. Like, one afternoon you'll turn it on and there's punk, and the next day you turn it on at the same time and there's classic rock, or maybe bluegrass. I hate it when it's bluegrass, but I listen to it anyway. You never know what you might learn."

So another thing Matthew Holler had given Kate was a new radio station to listen to. At first she hadn't liked K-DUCK very much. She'd sit on her bed and listen, but a lot of times she didn't know what she was listening to, and there was something about the songs that didn't exactly belong in her room. It was weird to listen to the pounding drums and screeching guitars and the singers going on about things Kate could hardly understand, and then glance over at her bookshelf and see her complete set of the Little House on the Prairie books and her My Little Pony collection, which she'd had since kindergarten. Kate's bedroom and K-DUCK were not a good mix-and-match combination, that much was clear.

But she kept listening. She figured out the K-DUCK system. All the announcers were college students, and there were different announcers every day. Their shows were two hours long, so if you tuned in at four and didn't like what you were hearing, you might as well turn off the radio until six.

Without realizing it, Kate started to like almost everything she heard, even the stuff that at first had sounded too fast and loud. You just had to get used to some music before you could appreciate it. It was hard to explain, but some of the loudest, fastest songs made her feel stronger, the way her boots did, the way playing guitar did. It was like the music got into your blood or something, she thought.

But her favorite K-DUCK show was on Thursday nights. The announcer was a girl named Lindsey, and her show was called *Girls with Guitars Unplugged*. Kate loved almost every song she heard. They were the kind of songs she was trying to write, songs that were about people doing things or thinking about things or just living their lives and sometimes being happy, sometimes sad.

One night Kate's mom walked into her bedroom while Kate was listening to *Girls with Guitars Unplugged* and doing her pre-algebra homework. Mrs. Faber opened her mouth to say something, but suddenly closed it again. She tilted her head toward Kate's boom box and listened for a few seconds. She sat down on Kate's bed and listened some more. When the song was over, she said, "I love Joni Mitchell. She's a genius."

"You know who that was singing that song?" Kate was amazed. She had no idea her mom had any musical knowledge whatsoever. She'd thought music was just background noise to her mom, something to keep a room from feeling too quiet.

"Oh, sure," Mrs. Faber replied. "I listened to *Blue* every day when I was in high school. It was the soundtrack to my life."

"Is *Blue* a Joni Mitchell CD?"

Mrs. Faber laughed. "Well, at the time it was a Joni Mitchell record," she said. "But yes, it's probably the greatest Joni Mitchell CD ever." Then Mrs. Faber paused and looked sad for a minute. "It just occurred to me that I really miss it."

The next day when Kate got home, her mom was in the kitchen frosting a cake in the shape of a duck. There was music on the CD player, but it wasn't Bach or Beethoven or any of those classical guys her mom usually listened to. After a minute, Kate recognized the voice.

"You got that Joni Mitchell CD, didn't you?" she asked her mom, who was humming under her breath as she painted an orange bill onto the duck cake.

"Yep," her mom answered. "This is the fif-teenth time I've listened to it today."

"You must be very happy," said Kate, reach-ing into the mixing bowl to snag a glob of frosting with her finger.

Mrs. Faber grinned wildly. "Ecstatic," she said. "I'd forgotten how music makes you feel. I mean, music that really gets inside of you."

So that was another thing from Matthew Holler, Kate figured. He'd given Kate K-DUCK, which in turn had given her mom Joni Mitchell back.

Kate knew she should really show Matthew her notebook. She knew it was her turn to share something. But her notebook was so new. It was still as fragile as a tiny bird in its new-ness. Almost anything could break its wings: a swift fall to the ground, the wrong word.

Kate would find something else to give Matthew. But not the notebook. Not yet.

The first thing Kate gave Matthew Holler was a rock.

It wasn't just any rock. It was the blue rock

she'd found on the beach when she was seven. It was round and mostly smooth and for a long time Kate had slept with it under her pillow for good luck.

She knew it was a good thing to give to Matthew, because in the three weeks that they had been friends she had learned that he was the sort of person who liked arrowheads and bird feathers and interesting-shaped sticks. She had learned that he liked old things better than new things and that what he wanted for Christmas this year was a wooden box he had seen on eBay. It reminded him of a box his grandfather had that had originally been his great-grandfather's.

"You should write a poem about that," Kate had told him, and Matthew said he might, seeming interested in the idea.

So when Kate was looking through her jewelry box for an old bracelet she'd forgotten about that she'd just remembered and found the blue rock, she knew immediately it was the sort of thing that Matthew would appreciate.

She gave it to him the next day before his Spanish test.

"For good luck," Kate told him, handing him the rock and feeling the tiniest twinge of regret that she was giving it away and it would never be hers again.

The twinge turned into a note of alarm when a girl Kate had never seen before walked by and said, "Hey, Mattie! Come talk to me at lunch!" The girl was pretty, much prettier than she was, Kate thought, and Matthew's eyes followed her as she walked down the hall.

"Who was that?" Kate asked, even as she insisted to herself that she shouldn't even care. It wasn't like she owned Matthew Holler. It wasn't like he couldn't be friends with other people.

Matthew shrugged. "Emily," he said. "Just somebody I know."

Then he held the rock up and examined it. "I can't believe you found this," he said. "I never find good rocks." Slipping it into his pocket, he slammed closed his locker door. "Are you sure you want to give it to me?"

Kate nodded. "Yeah. I just wanted you to have something that was, I don't know, good."

Matthew grinned. "I like getting stuff that's good. Mostly what people give me are T-shirts and socks. It's pretty depressing."

"Yeah, whatever happened to toys?" Kate said. "Even if we are too old for them, I guess."

They walked down the hall together. When Kate reached her classroom, she said good-bye and hurried to her desk, pulling her new notebook and pen out of her backpack.

Roca, she wrote, and then, *azul*.

Bella, she wrote, saying it softly under her breath. *"Bella."*

"La roca azul esta bella," Matthew had said right before they'd reached her class. *"Gracias."*

The blue rock is beautiful, he'd said.

Thank you.

Sometimes it seemed to Kate that her life was all about being friends with Matthew Holler, but it really wasn't. For instance, she was also becoming friends with Lorna, who Kate liked because Lorna was an intellectual and a writer and didn't like to talk about boys and who had a crush on who. Kate did not want to talk about boys or about being friends with Matthew Holler. She thought that too many words might ruin things. So in that regard, Lorna was the perfect person for her right now.

What Lorna liked to talk about most of all was food. Food was to Lorna what music was to Matthew Holler. She brought interesting lunches to school and shared them with Kate: burritos and chimichangas, curry and naan bread, Greek salads with black olives and feta cheese. Lorna made her lunches herself. "My mom hates to cook," she told Kate. "I do all the cooking in my family. My mom pays me twenty-five dollars a week to make dinner."

"You get paid to make dinner?" Kate asked.

Lorna shrugged. "What can I say? I'm a great cook. If things don't work out for me as a writer, I'll probably end up being a chef."

Kate and Lorna had started eating lunch together almost every day. Sometimes they talked, sometimes they read. Sometimes Lorna read to Kate from the novel she was writing. It was a story told from the point of view of a cat who was actually a ghost cat and had helped out on the Underground Railroad during the 1800s. Kate thought it was a pretty good story so far, though secretly she wondered how much help a cat could have been transporting slaves from the South to Canada. She'd known a few cats in her life, and they'd never struck her as the do-gooder types.

One day Lorna showed up in the cafeteria looking serious. This was unusual. Lorna normally looked like she found everything in the world particularly hilarious and couldn't wait to let you in on the joke. But now she wore a slight frown. She looked a little confused to Kate, like she wasn't sure about something.

"What's wrong?" Kate asked her. "Do you feel okay?"

Lorna sat down without saying anything. She didn't pull her lunch bag out of her backpack the way she typically did the second she sat down, making a big show out of unpacking it, explaining what each item was and how it was made. It worried Kate that Lorna was just sitting there, not unpacking, not talking.

"Did something bad happen?" Kate asked. "Because if it did, you could tell me."

Lorna let out her breath in a big rush. "Okay, I'm just going to say it. On my way here, I saw Matthew waiting outside the principal's office, and he looked upset, like something bad was going on."

"Maybe he's sick," Kate said, a stream of nervous energy suddenly rushing through her. What if something horrible had happened? What if Matthew needed her to be there with him right now? Should she go? She didn't have a hall pass, but she didn't care if she got in trouble, not if Matthew needed her help.

"I don't think so," said Lorna. "I mean, that's not what things seemed like."

Kate knew there was something Lorna wasn't saying. She leaned in toward her. "Tell me. Tell me what you're not telling me."

Lorna pursed her lips, like the words she was holding back were sour as lemons. "Okay, listen. I know you guys are just friends, so this isn't a big deal or anything. But he was sitting there with this girl. I don't know who she was, but she was sitting really close to him and saying that getting caught skipping wasn't such a big deal and they'd hardly get into any trouble for it at all."

"Matthew got caught skipping?" Kate sat back in her seat. "With a girl?"

"Yeah, and she's really pretty." Lorna smacked her hand over her mouth. "I'm sorry! I didn't mean to say that part."

Kate sat up straight. She refused to get upset over this. "It's okay. It was probably Emily, this girl he's friends with. He's got lots of friends."

"Yeah, no big deal, you're right," Lorna said, smiling weakly. "Besides, it's not like you guys are boyfriend-girlfriend or anything. You're just really good friends."

"That's right," said Kate. "That's just how it is."

Kate did not go to Creative Writing Club that afternoon, even though she had a draft of a new song she'd wanted to get feedback on. After the last bell, she got on the bus and took a seat at the back. She wanted to be alone and stare out of the window. She thought if she could just stare out the window for a long time without being interrupted, everything would make sense to her. She would suddenly understand why her good friend Matthew Holler, who was just her good friend and who she was not in love with, skipped class with Emily and hadn't said one word to her about it, even though they'd talked that morning before third period.

He could have mentioned it, Kate thought. He could have let me know what was going on in his life.

Someone sat down next to her. Kate looked up. Matthew?

Marylin.

"I have a dentist appointment at four," Marylin said, arranging her backpack at her feet. "I don't know why my mom can't make appointments during school like everyone else's mom does. Now I have to miss cheerleading practice, which means I get demerits."

"Doesn't your mom work?" Kate asked, forgetting to be irritated that Marylin was interrupting her staring-out-the-window time.

"Yeah, I know, but you'd think she'd like the excuse of taking some time off," Marylin said. She pulled the elastic out of her hair and began redoing her ponytail.

"Maybe her boss would give her demerits," Kate pointed out. "I think it's different taking time off when you're actually getting paid to be somewhere."

"Be on my mom's side, why don't you?" said Marylin, giving her ponytail one last tug. "Anyway, I saw your boyfriend in the office today. He looked like he was in a lot of trouble."

"I don't have a boyfriend," Kate said. "I only have friends, some of whom are boys. Besides, I think he has a girlfriend. I mean, one who's not me. At least that's what it sounds like. This friend of mine saw them waiting together after they got caught skipping."

Marylin looked shocked. "Did you know about her?"

"It doesn't matter," Kate said. She held up her fingers and began examining her calluses. They were an interesting color, somewhere between yellow and clear. "We weren't going together or anything. Doesn't the word 'friends' mean anything anymore?"

"To be honest, I'm really not sure," Marylin said. She turned and looked at Kate. "Do you ever miss it? Being all-the-time friends, like we used to be?"

Kate thought about this. It was hard to think about being friends with someone when you were in fourth or fifth grade, and trying to translate that friendship into seventh-grade terms. Part of the reason she and Marylin had been best friends for so long was that they lived close to each other and they were both basically nice people. They'd never had a lot of stuff in common, but when you're nine, it doesn't really matter all that much.

But when you're twelve, Kate thought, it matters more, liking the same things. She was glad, for instance, to have a friend like Lorna, who liked to write and read as much as Kate did. And, with a pang, she realized it was nice to have a friend like Matthew Holler, who understood about guitars and smooth blue rocks that were beautiful and felt good in your pocket.

That's not what she said, though. What she said was, "Yeah, I miss it."

And then Marylin laid her head on Kate's shoulder for a second, and Kate did everything she could not to cry.

That night Kate sat in the kitchen, listening to Joni Mitchell sing and writing down words in her notebook with her indigo blue pen. Her mom was looking through cookbooks and taking notes for a cake she was supposed to make for a bar mitzvah the following weekend.

Icicles, Kate wrote, copying words from the song that was playing. *Birthday clothes. Sorrow.*

"What's this song about, anyway?" she asked her mom. "Who's Little Green?"

"Little Green is the child Joni Mitchell gave up for adoption," her mom told her, flipping through the pages of her cookbook. "This is a song she wrote about it. When someone told me that this song was true, I couldn't stop crying, it was so sad."

Kate stared at her mom. She couldn't believe she was actually telling her something so interesting and grown-up. "I wish I could write a song like this," she said. Then, seeing her mom's shocked expression, she added, "I mean, a song that's as good as this one. Not one about me giving up a baby for adoption."

Mrs. Faber frowned. "Promise me, Kate, whatever you do, that you will not start having interesting experiences just for the sake of writing about them."

Kate held up her fingers in the Girl Scout salute. "I promise."

When the phone rang, Kate didn't bother picking up, since the phone was always for Tracie, and for once, Tracie was actually home to answer the phone herself. So it was a surprise when a moment later, Tracie called down from her room, "Kate! It's for you! And don't hog the phone all night!"

Kate grabbed the phone off the kitchen counter and turned down the volume on Joni Mitchell. Maybe it was Lorna, she thought as she hit the talk button, though Lorna was more of an instant messenger than a phoner.

She wasn't prepared at all to hear Matthew Holler's voice on the other end of the line.

"I think my big mistake today was leaving the blue rock at home," he said after she'd said hello, not even saying who he was, though Kate knew as soon as she'd heard him breathing. "Usually I put it in my pocket first thing in the morning, since it's good luck, but I was late and my mom was yelling, so I forgot."

"Are you in a lot of trouble?" Kate asked, forgetting that her mom was in the room, though she remembered as soon as her mom started hissing, "Who's in trouble? Who is it?" from across the kitchen.

"It's not so bad," said Matthew. "Three days of morning and after-school detention. It's the first time I ever got caught."

Kate moved out into the hallway, away from her mom's ears. "Do you skip a lot?" she asked in a half whisper.

"Not a lot," Matthew said. "But sometimes. Sometimes I think I'll go crazy if I have to sit at a desk for one more second. I don't do anything bad when I skip. I just like to walk around the neighborhoods near school and listen to my iPod. It clears my head."

What about Emily, Kate wanted to ask. *Does she always skip with you, or just every once in a while?*

But she didn't ask. Because she didn't want to know about Emily.

La roca azul esta bella, she thought.

Matthew Holler esta bello.

Do you ever miss it? she wanted to ask. *Being all-the-time friends?*

Except Matthew Holler had only been her friend since they'd met in Creative Writing Club, even if it seemed like a lifetime to Kate. A lifetime of guitars and radio stations, wooden boxes and crooked sticks. A lifetime of blue rocks that in a poem you would call stones.

She would never, ever tell anyone that she loved him.

"So, do you want to hear some stuff I've been writing down in my notebook?" she asked, walking back into the kitchen and taking a seat across from her mom. "I mean, like words and ideas for poems?"

"Yeah, that would be great," Matthew said. "And then I was thinking maybe we could play guitar together."

"You want to play guitar together on the phone?"

Across the table, Mrs. Faber giggled.

"Yeah, sure, why not?" Matthew asked. "You have anything against playing guitar over the phone?"

"No, I guess not," said Kate. "But first the words, okay, Matthew?"

"Okay," Matthew said.

"Here goes, then," Kate said, picking up her notebook and opening it. She took a deep breath.

"Blue," she said, her voice catching just a little.

"Cashmere", she continued.

"Icicles, birthday clothes, sorrow."

The whole time her mom looking at her.

The whole time her mom reaching out her hands.

※ † ※ ※ ※ ※ † ※ ※ ※ ※ ※ † ※ ※ ※ ※ † ※ ※ ※ ※ † ※ ※ ※

everything in the world

After Marylin was elected Student Government representative, walking into school first thing in the morning became a brand-new experience. She did not automatically check her reflection in the media center window, which she passed as soon as she entered the building, and she resisted the impulse to rush into the girls' bathroom next to the science lab to touch up her strawberry Lip Smacker lip gloss before heading to her locker. It wasn't that she didn't care about being pretty anymore, it was just that she had a different idea about herself all of the sudden. She was a person who, yes, was pretty, but she was also serious. She had business to take care of.

It was clear that Mazie did not like the new Marylin one bit.

"Do you know how boring you've become?" she asked the morning after Marylin's second Student Government meeting. Marylin had been telling Mazie and Ashley about how a group of eighth-grade representatives were lobbying for more vegetarian entrées in the cafeteria, and how they thought that the administration was conspiring against them to save money. Marylin had been shocked by the eighth graders' claim that Principal Carter-Juarez was secretly plotting with the food services people to keep eggplant Parmesan and tofu burgers off the cafeteria's menu.

Marylin blinked a few times after Mazie accused her of being boring. Had she been boring? Was she talking too much? Was it possible that other people did not find politics as interesting as Marylin now did?

She looked closely at Mazie's and Ashley's faces and realized that, yes, it was possible not everyone found the ins and outs, ups and downs of Brenner P. Dunn Middle School's Student Government all that fascinating.

"Sorry," she mumbled. "I didn't mean to hog the conversation."

Mazie leaned toward Marylin and poked her in the shoulder with her finger. "Your job is to get us new uniforms. Don't start thinking it's to make the world safe for vegans."

Marylin rubbed her shoulder where Mazie had poked her. She stood there rubbing it for several minutes while Mazie and Ashley started to describe to each other in great detail what the perfect cheerleading uniform would look like, both agreeing that it was essential that belly buttons be visible at all times.

When she saw Kate and Matthew Holler walking down the hall, Marylin broke away from Mazie and Ashley with a quick "Gotta run" and trotted toward them. "Hey, you guys," she called. "I need to ask you something."

Matthew looked at Marylin curiously, his head tilted slightly to one side. "Ask away," he said with a sudden grin that made Marylin automatically understand what Kate saw in him.

"Uh, okay, what was I going to ask you?" Marylin fell into step beside Kate and nudged her. The nudge was supposed to say, *Are you guys an item or what?* but Kate just rolled her eyes at Marylin in a way that let it be known she found the whole subject irritating. "Oh, yeah. Vegetarian cafeteria—are you for it or against it?"

"All the way vegetarian?" Kate asked. "I mean, some vegetarian stuff would be great, but it wouldn't be fair if there weren't any cheeseburgers. A lot of people like cheeseburgers."

Matthew held up his hand. "Personally, I'm for cheeseburgers. Though I respect vegetarians. My cousin Ryan is a vegetarian because he refuses to eat anything he wouldn't kill, and since he can't imagine killing a cow or a pig, he basically doesn't eat meat."

"How about a deer?" Kate said. "Would he kill a deer?"

"That's the funny thing," Matthew answered, draping an arm around Kate's shoulders. "He has killed a deer. He lives out in the country, and my uncle's really into hunting, and one time last year Ryan killed a deer. But after they cooked it and everything, he didn't like the way it tasted."

"That's ironic," said Marylin, then wished she hadn't, because she wasn't sure if she 100 percent knew what "ironic" meant, and maybe it didn't mean what she thought it meant at all.

But Kate and Matthew both laughed, and Kate said, "No kidding," and Marylin suddenly felt okay.

What an interesting experience, she thought later, as she was taking out her homework folder in math. To have a conversation and feel okay about it afterward.

Quite frankly, Marylin hadn't known that was possible.

Student Government meetings were held Monday nights in the media center. Marylin had expected to be bored half the time, because Clarissa Sharp, who had been a representative the year before, had told her there were a lot of budget discussions and debates over whether or not the Chess Club should get to use a school van to go to tournaments at other schools. Before Marylin went to the first meeting, she'd tucked a copy of the most recent *Seventeen* in her back pouch, thinking she could sneak-read it if the meeting got supremely dull.

To her surprise, Marylin found all of it interesting, from the explanation of how to use *Robert's Rules of Order* to the line-by-line review of the activities budget. It didn't hurt that the Student Government president, Benjamin Huddle, was cute in a geeky sort of way. Marylin wondered if she could somehow tactfully suggest that he get contact lenses and trade out his button-down shirts for T-shirts. It would, in her opinion, make a huge difference.

There were two other seventh-grade representatives. One was Alison Crabtree, a soccer player with one of those outgoing personalities that made it impossible to know if she liked you or not, because she acted like everyone in the world was her best friend, and how could that be? The other representative was a boy named Saunders Peck. Saunders Peck was known for being smarter than everyone else and very ambitious, but if he had an actual personality, Marylin had never heard about it. She had tried to be nice to him at first, but he'd hardly responded at all, just sort of sniffed at her. She wondered if he thought she was beneath him because she was a cheerleader and not some rocket scientist.

So it came as a surprise that, after the second meeting in December, Saunders Peck asked Marylin if she would like to accompany him to the Student Organizations Holiday Extravaganza that weekend.

"It's at the Holiday Inn on Bryson Boulevard," he told her in the hallway as they walked toward the front door. "Music, snacks, some sort of moronic entertainment—according to my brother, who was Student Government president a few years ago. He's the one who would drive us. Dan, that is. My brother. He goes to Parkside High School now."

"Is he Student Government president there?" Marylin asked, trying to stall for time. She did not in any way want to go to the

Holiday Extravaganza with Saunders Peck, but she needed a nice way to say no and was having a hard time coming up with one.

Saunders scowled. "No, but that's because they're all idiots. Oh sure, it's supposed to be one of the best high schools in the state, but if you're not popular, forget about running for office there."

Marylin thought this was probably not a great time to turn Saunders down. "I'd better check to see if my mom's out front," she said, turning toward the school entrance. "She gets mad if I make her wait."

Scurrying to the front door, her fingers crossed that her mom's car would be at the curb, Marylin tried desperately to come up with a plan. There was no possible way she was going to go to the Holiday Extravaganza with Saunders Peck. First of all, as a middle-school cheerleader, there was only so much she could get away with. Being friends with Kate Faber? Acceptable, if not preferable. Taking Student Government seriously, even if her real role there was to make things better for middle-school cheerleaders? Pushing it. Going on a date with Saunders Peck, a boy who, while academically and politically successful, was not actually that cute and by the time high school rolled around might drop off into the abyss of unpopularity?

Forget about it.

Besides, Marylin didn't think she liked him very much, which had nothing to do with her being a middle-school cheerleader, just her own personal feelings. Shouldn't her feelings count for something? She didn't have to say yes just because somebody asked her to do something, did she? She didn't always have to be nice just because she was a nice person.

It would have been useful if her mom's car had been parked out front, but it wasn't, which meant Marylin was going to have to take a deep breath, go back inside, and tell Saunders kindly, but firmly, that she did not want to go to the Holiday Extravaganza with him.

Fortunately, at the last second she noticed Benjamin Huddle standing over by the statue of the Brenner P. Dunn Middle School wildcat, the school mascot, his backpack on his back, both straps on his shoulders, his blue jacket zipped all the way up, so that he looked like a little kid.

"Oh, hi, Benjamin," Marylin said, a little zing of excitement zipping through her. She didn't know if she was excited because now she didn't have to go back inside, or if it had more to do with the fact that standing out in the cold all zipped up, Benjamin Huddle was cuter than she'd ever realized. Marylin wondered if he had a girlfriend. "Are you waiting for your mom?"

That sounded stupid, Marylin thought, like a question you'd ask a preschooler. But Benjamin didn't seem to mind. He walked over to Marylin and said, "My dad, actually. My mom teaches at the Arts Center on Monday nights."

"What does she teach?" Marylin asked, hoping her questions would make this bloom into an actual conversation.

"Drawing for kids," said Benjamin. "Not little kids. Kids our age who are sort of advanced."

"I wish I could draw," Marylin said, setting her back pouch on the sidewalk. "But all I can do are stick people."

Benjamin laughed. "Yeah, me too. It's a huge disappointment to my mom. She wants all my brothers and sisters to be Picassos or something."

"How many brothers and sisters do you have?"

"Four, if you can believe it. I'm the oldest, with the least artistic talent."

"But you're good at other stuff," Marylin insisted. "I mean, you're a great Student Government president."

"Do you really think so?" Benjamin asked, stepping even closer. "I worry that we're not getting enough done."

"Are you kidding? I can't believe how much we've done in just three meetings," Marylin said. "I don't have much experience or anything, but I've been pretty amazed at all the stuff we've covered so far."

Cars began streaming into the school driveway, headlights bouncing against the wildcat.

"Oh, there's my mom," Marylin said, spotting the silver minivan at the end of the line.

Benjamin scanned the line of cars. "Yeah, I see my dad, too." He shifted the weight of his pack, then turned to her. "Uh, Marylin, I was wondering—"

He was interrupted by Saunders Peck, who jumped up beside him. "What's taking you so long?" he asked Marylin, sounding irritated. "I've been waiting in there for at least three minutes."

"Oh, Saunders, hi." Marylin's voice sounded fakey to her ears. It sounded like a voice in a TV show filled with bad actors. "Um, about that Extravaganza, what I meant to tell you was—"

"What?" Saunders asked in an impatient tone of voice. "What did you mean to tell me?"

"I'm already going with someone else?" Marylin looked at Benjamin, who appeared confused by this turn of events. "Right, Benjamin?"

A headlight shined in Benjamin's eyes, and Marylin could see that he suddenly got it.

"Yeah, sorry, Saunders. Marylin's going with me."

Saunders gave Marylin a stricken look. "You might have said something inside, you know. I guess this is like a joke to you, right? Like maybe other people don't have feelings?"

Marylin and Benjamin watched Saunders stomp off toward the car in front of the pickup line. "Wow," Benjamin said. "That guy has some anger management problems."

"I don't know, I think he's just kind of embarrassed," said Marylin, feeling terrible that she hadn't handled things better. Okay, so there was no way she was going to have said yes, but she should have found a direct way to tell him no. She should have pretended she was Kate and said something straight off the bat. Now she felt like a really rotten person.

But at the same time she felt great. She looked at Benjamin, who really was cute, and actually kind of tall. And presidential, Marylin thought. A little goofy, but definitely presidential.

"So, anyway, my mom or dad will have to

drive us and everything," Benjamin said, sounding apologetic. "Because, well, I don't have my license." He paused. "That sounded stupid, didn't it? You wouldn't actually expect me to have my license."

Marylin laughed. Was it possible that this cute, presidential-looking boy worried as much as she did about saying dumb things? "It didn't sound stupid. And it's okay about your parents driving. I don't mind."

"Thanks," Benjamin said. He turned toward his dad's car, then turned back again. "By the way, did I ask you, or did you ask me?"

"I think we kind of asked each other," said Marylin.

Benjamin grinned. "Cool."

Yeah, Marylin thought, walking over to where her mom was parked. Cool.

Here was the problem: The Extravaganza was on Saturday night, and Marylin was supposed to stay at her dad's. Normally it would be okay, under the circumstances, for Marylin to come back home late Saturday afternoon, so that

Benjamin's parents wouldn't have to drive all the way to her dad's apartment to pick her up for the party. But on this particular Saturday night, her mom was going on a pre-Christmas visit to Aunt Tish's house, which was three hours away. Marylin made the case that she should be able to spend the night by herself in her own house, but her parents weren't buying it.

"Why don't you see if you could spend the night at Kate's house?" her mom had asked, which would have been a good idea, only Kate's family was going to be out of town that weekend too. "So what about Mazie? Or another one of your cheerleader friends?" her mom had then suggested reasonably. "There's got be somebody who can help you out."

Thinking over her options, Marylin realized she did not want to stay over at Mazie's house. Mazie would not be supportive. She would have a list of at least twenty-five things that were wrong with Benjamin Huddle, even if he was Student Government president. She would make fun of Marylin before Benjamin picked her up, and she would make fun of Benjamin after he dropped Marylin off.

This was not how Marylin wanted her first date to be. She loved the idea of spending the night with a friend so that they could go over the date in detail afterward, but it needed to be a nice friend, a supportive friend, a friend who would be excited for Marylin. Marylin imagined the two of them—whoever the friend might be—wrapped up in bathrobes and sipping hot chocolate as they discussed everything that had happened, from the minute that Benjamin knocked on the door to the minute he dropped her off after the Extravaganza was over.

Mazie was not that kind of friend.

To be honest, neither was Kate, Marylin had to admit, although Kate would be a hundred times better than Mazie. Kate could appreciate the appeal of Benjamin Huddle, unlike Mazie, who only appreciated eighth-grade football players.

And then it came to her. Ruby Santiago. Marylin had been dying to spend the night at

Ruby's all fall, just waiting for the chance for the two of them to bond. Of course, Ruby was not the sort of person you asked to spend the night. You had to wait for her to ask you. But this was a special occasion, and just the opportunity Marylin had been looking for.

"Saturday night?" Ruby had asked when Marylin brought up the subject of a sleepover. "I guess that would be okay. I'll have to ask my mom, though. She doesn't like it when we invite people without checking with her first."

That was Tuesday morning. By Tuesday afternoon, home after cheerleading practice, Marylin was a jumble of nervous excitement waiting for Ruby's call. Ruby had promised to call before dinner. Marylin tried to do her homework, the phone on the bed beside her, but she couldn't concentrate. Outside her window, the afternoon darkened into evening, and inside, the smell of meat loaf drifted up the stairs, mixing with Marylin's excitement and making her feel a little sick. Call, call, call, she ESP'd to Ruby, but the only time the phone rang, it was the library, a computerized voice informing Marylin that her mother had three items overdue.

By eight, Ruby still hadn't called, and Marylin wondered if she should call Ruby. But she knew this went against middle-school cheerleading protocol. The second prettiest cheerleader did not call the prettiest cheerleader—it was always the other way around, no exceptions.

Marylin waited until midnight before completely giving up hope. In the morning, groggy eyed, she made her way to Ruby's locker, where Ruby stood with Ashley and Mazie. "I thought you were going to call last night," she said to Ruby, and immediately realized that this was a mistake. As nice as Ruby was, you still didn't reprimand her, especially not in front of other people.

"Was I?" Ruby asked, sounding both innocent and imperial at the same time. "Gosh, Marylin, I guess I forgot. But I did ask my mom about Saturday and she said no. I forgot that it's the youth group Christmas party that night. My mom never lets me skip church stuff."

"Mine either," Ashley chimed in. "If it has to do with church, I have to be there."

Ruby smiled at Ashley serenely. "Your mom sounds a lot like mine."

Ashley nodded several times like a happy puppy. Marylin thought she was going to throw up. She definitely wasn't going to ask Ashley if she could spend the night at her house. But who was she going to ask? For a popular person, she was starting to feel sort of pathetic.

The idea came to her in language arts, but she rejected it immediately. Even though she and Rhetta were friendly now, chatting in the minutes before their classes started, Rhetta showing Marylin her latest drawings, Marylin offering the occasional story idea, that wasn't the same as them being friends. Besides, what could spending the night at Rhetta's house be like? Marylin imagined walls painted black, cats slithering around, a crow perched in an ornate birdcage. Marylin would probably be too scared to fall asleep.

But the fact was, it was Wednesday afternoon. If she didn't have something lined up soon, then Benjamin's parents would have to drive to her dad's to get her, and they'd have to drive all the way back afterward, or else Marylin's dad would have to drive her, and Petey would be sitting in the backseat with Marylin and Benjamin, and that was just too unromantic for words.

Rhetta, she decided with a sigh, was her only hope.

"Yeah, sure, no problem," Rhetta replied, not acting like she had to think about it or ask her mom first. For someone who dressed all in black and didn't seem to have many friends, she sounded like having Marylin spend the night was a run-of-the-mill event. "My mom buys microwave popcorn by the caseload, so we can hang out all night eating popcorn and watching TV. It'll be cool."

Marylin stared at Rhetta, reassessing her. Was it possible that under that gloom-and-doom exterior, Rhetta Mayes was actually a normal twelve-year-old girl who liked popcorn and sleepovers?

Who knew?

"So what were you and Miss Ghoul talking about?" Mazie asked after language arts. "She seemed pretty excited over something."

"She's, uh, interested in Student Government stuff," Marylin stammered. "You know, all that vegetarian stuff. She's against meat."

"It figures," said Mazie, rolling her eyes in Rhetta's general direction. "I don't know why they let freaks like her go to school."

"Somebody's a freak just because they don't eat meat?" Marylin asked, surprising herself. She'd never talked back to Mazie before. It was sort of great and sort of terrifying at the same time. She decided to keep going, even though she had no idea whether Rhetta ate meat or not. "That's pretty, I don't know, narrow-minded, don't you think?"

Mazie raised an eyebrow. "Let me know when you're ready to get off your high horse, Miss Priss. And you might think twice about the way you're talking to me. If I felt like it, I could make your life pretty miserable."

You're already making my life miserable, Marylin wanted to say. But she didn't. One of these days, she was going to start telling Mazie what she actually thought 100 percent of the time. Maybe that would be her New Year's resolution. In the upcoming year, she would be a truth teller. All the time, not just when she forgot to lie in order to get along.

That gave her two more weeks of being friends with Mazie. Because when Marylin started telling the truth, Mazie wasn't going to put up with it, not for a second.

"If you wanted, I could put some makeup on you."

Marylin took a few steps back from Rhetta. "Well, um, I don't know. You and I sort of have different styles."

Rhetta laughed. "I won't try to make you look like me. I'll just make you look more like you."

"Well, okay, I guess." Marylin looked at the

clock on Rhetta's bedside table. She had forty-five minutes before Benjamin was going to pick her up. If Rhetta's makeup job was horrible, or even the least bit not cute, she still had time to wash it off. "Just in case you were wondering, I prefer the natural look. My mom doesn't like me wearing too much makeup. Mostly just lip gloss and maybe a little blush."

"Don't worry, I know what I'm doing," Rhetta said, rummaging through a box in her closet. You could tell that the Mayeses had just moved in, the way half of Rhetta's stuff was still packed up in cardboard boxes scattered around her room. "Do you think my dad would let me do all the makeup for the Christmas pageant if I didn't?"

Marylin had to admit that it was unlikely that Mr. Mayes—make that Reverend Mayes—would trust Rhetta to put makeup on Mary and the angels if he thought she was going to turn them into witches and vampires and other creatures from the dark side. Still, you'd think he might worry about it just the teeniest bit.

Though, come to think of it, Reverend

Mayes didn't seem like the worrying type. "You can call me Jack, all the youth at church do," Reverend Mayes had told Marylin when Rhetta introduced them. "Actually, they call me Pastor Jack, and if you're more comfortable with that, that's fine."

At the church Marylin went to, they called the minister Father Markham. Marylin wasn't sure what his first name was, or if he even had one. She couldn't imagine him ever dressed like Reverend Mayes was, in a pale blue polo shirt, jeans, and running shoes, and she couldn't even begin to picture him sporting a little goatee on his chin. Marylin thought Reverend Mayes's goatee was sort of cute. In fact, Reverend Mayes himself was sort of cute. But how did someone as clean-cut as he was end up with a daughter like Rhetta?

"Does your dad mind, you know, the way you dress and everything?" Marylin asked Rhetta as she applied eye shadow to the crease of Marylin's right eye. "I mean, it's not very church-y."

"I think it bugs my mom, but not my dad,"

Rhetta said, breathing pepperoni pizza breath into Marylin's face as she dabbed on the eye makeup. "My dad is a pretty contemporary guy. Like, we don't have a choir at church, we have a band, you know? And there's a youth band too, and the bass player has a pierced lip. My dad says clothes don't matter and tattoos don't matter. All that matters is what's inside."

Marylin peered at Rhetta in the mirror, thinking that it was absolutely impossible to know someone until you'd been in their house, and even then, you could never know them all the way. Everyone, it seemed to Marylin, had a part of them that stayed a mystery. She couldn't figure out if she liked that idea or if it was a little scary, like there was a part of you that would always be alone. "So do you mind, like, having to go to church all the time and that stuff?"

"It's not so bad." Rhetta took a step back and examined her work. "It's part of my job description, right? But that doesn't mean I have to be all angelic and holy or anything. How boring would that be?"

Earlier that evening, at the dinner table, it had kind of shocked Marylin when Reverend Mayes led them in prayer over the pizza box at dinner, but what was even more shocking was that Rhetta had bowed her head and not seemed the least bit embarrassed about it.

While they were eating, Reverend and Mrs. Mayes ("Oh, just call me Miss Charlene, all the kids do") had asked Marylin questions about the middle school, which they told her was twice the size of Rhetta's last school, and they asked her questions about herself. Mrs. Mayes had gotten all excited when she found out Marylin was a cheerleader.

"I was a cheerleader!" she'd exclaimed. "I loved it. You know what always bothered me, though? No one ever recognized that cheerleading is really a sport. You have to be an athlete to be a cheerleader. I think people see that more now, but when I was in high school, everybody took cheerleaders for granted. We were just a lot of pretty faces back then."

Marylin could see that Mrs. Mayes had probably been a good cheerleader. There was something naturally bouncy about her, for one thing. Also, she seemed genuinely cheerful. She'd chattered on through dinner about this and that, saying funny and silly things that made Rhetta and her little brother Charlie moan and groan and giggle.

"Now, Rhetta was the cutest little baby," Mrs. Mayes told Marylin. "But boy, was she fussy. She had colic her first year. Charlie here is lucky he ever got born, because, honey, after that first year with Rhetta screaming all day and night, I swore up and down that one baby was all I was going to have."

Then she leaned over and gave Rhetta a kiss on the cheek. "But you turned out to be simply wonderful, didn't you, sweetheart? The cutest two-year-old that ever was, and you've stayed cute ever since."

Rhetta rolled her eyes and mumbled, "Yeah, right, Mom," but Marylin could tell she really didn't mind all that much.

"Your parents are nice," Marylin told Rhetta now. "They're really comfortable to be around."

Rhetta blew some blush powder off a brush

and began swabbing Marylin's cheeks with it. "Yeah, they're okay. They're way too strict, though. I do something wrong, *boom*! I'm on restriction for a month. Like this time last summer, when me and my friend stayed out in the backyard talking until midnight, only my parents thought I was in bed. When they realized I wasn't, they called everybody they could think of trying to find me, and the whole time I was out back. Man, were they mad."

"Just wait until that happens to you." Reverend Mayes stood in the doorway to Rhetta's room. "Then you'll understand why we were so upset."

He turned to Marylin. "I don't know what time your folks are picking you up tomorrow, but I hope you'll consider coming to church with us. Doesn't matter what you wear. We don't care too much about clothes at our church, do we, Rhetta?"

"Well, Mom finally made people take off their baseball caps during the service," Rhetta pointed out.

"You have to admit, baseball caps in church

is pushing it," Reverend Mayes said. "But otherwise, just about anything goes. If you're afraid my sermon will be too boring, you can help Rhetta in the nursery. She has a heart for the little ones."

"Okay," said Marylin. "I might be able to go."

Reverend Mayes smiled. "Fantastic! We'd love to have you. Heck, call your folks, ask them to meet us there for the service!"

Marylin looked at the floor. "Uh, my parents are divorced," she said, ashamed to admit that to a minister. "So they don't go to stuff together anymore."

"That's okay," Reverend Mayes said kindly. "One or the other could come, or they could both come and sit on different sides. We've got some folks who do that." He stepped out into the hallway, then turned back and smiled at Marylin. "Everybody's broken, sweetie. God helps us get put back together."

After her dad had walked down the hall, Rhetta said, "Excuse all the God talk around here. It gets old after a while."

"It's okay," Marylin said. "I don't really mind it."

Rhetta stepped back and peered at Marylin. "Well, that's good news. The even better news? You look fabulous."

Marylin turned to the mirror to see, almost afraid to look. She closed her eyes, and when she opened them, she let out a little gasp. She was—well, beautiful. What had Rhetta done? You could hardly tell that Marylin had makeup on at all, but at the same time, she'd been totally transformed.

"I look like someone in a movie," she told Rhetta. "I can hardly believe it's me."

"You look exactly like yourself, but with maybe a little more of what's good on the inside shining through."

Marylin laughed. "I think you have a heart for makeup."

"I do," Rhetta said. "I really do. Well, what I have a heart for is beautiful stuff. Like art and music and fairies. I like everything that's beautiful."

Marylin was puzzled. On the one hand, sure,

she had seen Rhetta's notebooks filled with fairies and magical creatures and beautiful forest ferns and arbors laced with flowers. On the other hand, she'd also seen Rhetta's wardrobe.

An idea suddenly hit Marylin with the force of a hurricane. If Rhetta could make her look beautiful, maybe she could make Rhetta look beautiful. Unlike Kate, Rhetta actually cared about beauty; she was just too stubborn to let her beautiful side out.

Marylin knew she'd have to be subtle, though. She'd have to make it seem like she and Rhetta were doing some sort of art project together.

A warning sounded in her brain: Becoming friends with Rhetta Mayes meant there were all sorts of people who wouldn't want to be friends with Marylin. Mazie, to start with, followed by Ashley, Ruby, and all the other middle-school cheerleaders.

So what, Marylin thought, trying to feel brave about it, though really, what she felt was nervous, like she was about to take a walk along the edge of a very high cliff.

I should get a pair of boots like Kate's, she thought, finally understanding why Kate wore those big, black clodhoppers. Shoes like that would hold you to the ground, keep you from falling. Then she giggled. You couldn't pay her to wear those boots. She had way too much fashion sense.

"Would you like to come over to my house sometime?" she asked Rhetta, making herself take the first step out onto the cliff. "You could see my room and meet my mom and stuff."

A blush spread across Rhetta's cheeks and nose. "Yeah, that would be awesome," she said, sounding pleased. "Maybe over Christmas break?"

"Sure," said Marylin, the thought of Christmas making her feel a little bit giddy. Just that afternoon, taking out the trash, she'd sensed the first little molecules of Christmas in the air, a crisp pine-tree smell, the promise of cookies sprinkled with red and green sugar. Now she found herself excited thinking of a periwinkle blue sweater she had that would look perfect on Rhetta. "We'll have fun."

Marylin might let Rhetta keep one or two black items in her wardrobe, but otherwise it was going to be a complete transformation.

"You know, you're really a lot different from how I thought you were when I first met you," Rhetta said. "You're much more of a real person."

Marylin nodded. "You're right," she said. "I am."

After only an hour laughing and talking at the Student Organizations Holiday Extravaganza, Marylin realized she had a heart for Benjamin Huddle.

Only she really wished he'd stop staring at her.

"I can't help it," he said after she complained. "You're so pretty, I have to stare."

"But that's not what's important about me," Marylin insisted, though she had to admit she'd be upset if Benjamin didn't think she was pretty, especially tonight. Still, it was weird to have someone look at you all the time, like you were a painting or a television screen.

Benjamin covered his eyes with his hands. "Okay, I'll stop looking. Let's talk. What do you want to talk about?"

"We could talk about school, I guess," said Marylin, feeling unsure about what the best topic of conversation would be. "Or maybe that's boring. I don't know. What's your favorite class?"

"History," Benjamin said, his hands still over his eyes. "Next question?"

Marylin giggled. "I think it's your turn to ask me a question. And it's not like you can't ever look at me. Just don't stare."

Benjamin put his hands down and blinked, like the light was hurting his eyes. "Well, what do you think about this amazing party?" he asked. "Do you like parties? Or are you more of a homebody? Or is that a stupid question to ask a cheerleader?"

"I like parties," Marylin said. "I like places where there are lots of people. But sometimes I like quiet, too. It just depends, I guess."

She looked out across the room. As parties went, this one wasn't the most exciting in the world. It wasn't as good as her Back-to-School party, with all the cheerleaders and football and soccer players. This party was for all the Student Government representatives, plus the Student Government officers and all the school club officers, all the kids who had been elected by other kids to run things. The boys here were quieter, skinnier, and they didn't mix very much with the girls, who stood in bouncy, eager groups by the food tables, giggling and occasionally pointing over to one cluster of boys or another.

Marylin wasn't sure that she fit in here. But she wasn't sure she fit in with the cheerleaders and the football and soccer players anymore either. She wanted to fit in somewhere, but where? Her home was broken now, and how could you fit into a broken place? She wished she could fit in with Kate, and sometimes she still did, but Kate was changing shape, it seemed to Marylin, and it was hard to know exactly how to fit in with her anymore. She liked Rhetta, but she knew they weren't a perfect fit, and she didn't know Benjamin well enough to know whether they fit together or not, though she hoped they did.

Marylin felt herself wobble a bit, like she'd gotten too close to the edge of the cliff and was about to tumble over. She reached out and grabbed Benjamin's hand, to steady herself.

"You okay?" he asked, tightening his hand around hers.

"Yeah, I'm okay," she told him. "Just, well, I don't know. Ask me another question."

"Okay, let's see." Benjamin got a serious expression on his face. "If you could have anything in the world for Christmas, what would it be?"

Marylin thought about this for a long time. She considered the clothes she'd like to have, thought about the iPhone with the hot-pink case Caitlin Moore had gotten for her birthday and the makeup kit she'd seen at Nordstrom's with forty-seven shades of eye shadow.

And then she thought about Benjamin and Kate, and her mom and dad and Petey. She thought about the middle-school cheerleaders and the soccer and football players. She thought about Student Government, and about how maybe next year she'd run for president, and she thought about Rhetta, picturing her with long, flowing red hair. She thought about a story she'd been meaning to write, one about a girl who saves a dog from the pound, and after that, she thought some more about the iPhone.

"Everything," Marylin answered finally. "I think I would like everything in the world."

"Kinda greedy, aren't you?" Benjamin laughed.

Marylin nodded. "You could say that. Is that terrible?"

"Terrible? No," Benjamin said. "Impossible? Probably."

Marylin sighed. That's what she'd been afraid of.

Rhetta was waiting at the front door when Benjamin's dad dropped Marylin off at the Mayeses' house. "All right, spill it," she said, ushering Marylin into the house. "How was Prince Charming? Did the glass slipper fit or what?"

They sat on Rhetta's bed. Marylin looked in the mirror and saw that her makeup had worn off, and she looked like her real self again, pretty, but also normal, and a little bit tired.

"We talked a lot," Marylin began. "Which was fun. He's pretty easy to talk to."

"Do you like him?" asked Rhetta. She raised an eyebrow. "I mean, really like him?"

Marylin nodded. "He's kind of this mix of regular and special, you know?"

"Just like you," Rhetta said. "That's exactly the way you are."

Marylin thought about this for a moment. "Maybe that's exactly how everyone is."

Rhetta shook her head. "Not me. I'm just special."

Marylin laughed, and Rhetta joined in, and before long they were laughing in big, gulping fits of laughter, the sort of laughter you couldn't stop once you got going, laughter that was about laughing and not whatever got you started laughing. Marylin's stomach began to hurt, and when Rhetta actually rolled off the bed, Marylin thought there was a chance she might break a rib, she was laughing so hard.

Finally the laughter slowed, and Marylin took in big breaths to steady herself. Rhetta lay on the floor, holding her stomach with one hand and wiping tears from her eyes with the other. It would have been nice if Kate was there, Marylin suddenly thought, and Petey. Kate and Petey could keep the laughter going, and they would probably laugh all night and keep saying funny things until somebody finally smothered them with pillows, which would make everyone laugh even harder.

Then I'd feel safe, Marylin thought, not sure what she meant by that, except that she imagined everybody's hands holding on to her, so that she wouldn't fall off the cliff, so that she could keep walking until she got to where she was going.

a christmas carol

It is Christmas Eve, and Petey McIntosh is still working out the physics of Santa Claus. Yesterday, the last day of school before the holidays, Gretchen Humboldt argued that his equation was incorrect, and he finally had to agree with her. He had used the Earth's circumference—24,901.55 miles—as the distance that Santa Claus had to fly in twenty-four hours, but as Gretchen noted, Santa doesn't fly in a straight line around the globe. He goes north and south and all over the place. So now Petey is trying different ways of figuring out the actual distance Santa Claus flies on Christmas Eve.

He and Gretchen are secret Santa believers, and they have spent much of the last two weeks of school by the swings, whispering facts to each other about reindeer, the North Pole, and the true identity of Mrs. Claus. Other kids started to tease them about being boyfriend and girlfriend, and Petey and Gretchen didn't argue with them. They knew it was better to be thought a romantic item than babies who still believed that a jolly old elf with a bag of toys slid down their chimneys every December 24.

Petey likes working on the Santa Claus problem. This way he doesn't have to think about the Mom and Dad problem, or the Christmas Will Be Different This Year but You'll Get Used to It problem. After dinner, Petey, his mom, and Marylin will meet Petey's dad at the Church of New Hope to see a Christmas pageant, and then Petey and Marylin will go to their dad's apartment and eat popcorn and watch *It's a Wonderful Life*, before hanging their stockings from the built-in bookshelf in the living room and going to bed.

Petey has convinced himself it doesn't matter that his dad's apartment doesn't have a fireplace. Santa Claus, Petey thinks, could land on the balcony and come through the sliding glass doors. As Gretchen Humboldt has pointed out, millions of kids all over the world live in houses without fireplaces. That Santa needs a fireplace to enter a house is a myth, in Gretchen's opinion.

It means a lot to Petey that Gretchen believes in Santa Claus too. He knows that if she didn't, he would have to give up Santa Claus once and for all. Belief in Santa Claus is not something you can hold on to all by yourself, especially not in fourth grade. Besides, Gretchen is right about everything, and if she said there wasn't a Santa Claus, then Petey would finally have to give up and admit the likelihood of an old man driving a sleigh filled with presents around the world in a twenty-four-hour period was not great.

But thanks to Gretchen, he doesn't have to. He can happily sit at the kitchen table, the smell of banana nut bread baking in the oven floating over him, the blinking Christmas tree lights reflected in the living-room window, and punch numbers into his calculator, working out the exact science of Christmas.

It is Christmas Eve, and Flannery sits on the couch in the living room, listening to her stepbrother Ellis go on and on about college and all the wild, out-of-control things he's been doing this semester. Flannery's stepdad, Stan, nods his head like crazy, as though he doesn't mind that instead of attending classes and studying, Ellis seems to be spending his college years taking spur-of-the-moment cross-country rides to see bands no one has ever heard of and running around the campus's main quad at three a.m. wrapping the lampposts with toilet paper. Stan seems to find it all too hilarious for words.

Flannery's mom walks into the room with the phone in her hand. "They can't find his luggage anywhere," she says to Stan. She turns to

Ellis. "They're doing everything to track it, honey. They think it probably flew on to Atlanta after you made your connection in Chicago."

Ellis shakes his head, like he can't believe how cruel the world is to him. "I don't care about the clothes," he says. "I can borrow some of Dad's clothes. But I need my guitar. If I go more than twenty-four hours without playing, it's like my hands get arthritis or something. All the tendons and stuff start tightening up."

Flannery's mom's face lights up with a smile. "Flannery has a guitar," she chirps. "You can play hers while we're waiting for yours to show up."

Ellis looks at Flannery. His expression is doubtful. "What kind of guitar do you have?"

"Electric," Flannery says. "Fender."

"More specific, please," Ellis says in a snotty tone of voice, like he is Mr. Guitar Expert of the Universe.

"Stratocaster, blue finish, medium-heavy strings."

"Yeah, whatever, okay," Ellis says, shrugging.

"I'll make do. The only Fender worth playing is a Telecaster, and Fenders suck in general. You want to play guitar? Get a Gibson, man. A Gibson Les Paul."

"Is that what you play, honey?" Flannery's mom asks, sitting down next to Stan on the couch and smiling brightly at her stepson.

Ellis turns away and mumbles, "I wish."

Flannery's mom turns to Flannery. "Go get Ellis your guitar, sweetie. I'd really love to hear him play."

"I can't," Flannery says. "Kate Faber has it."

"Then go get it from Kate," her mom says, the bright and shiny smile still pasted on her face. "I'm sure she's not using it."

Shrugging into her jacket, Flannery wonders how her mom can be sure Kate's not playing her guitar at this very moment. It's the sort of thing her mom says all the time, as though you can wipe away problems or stress or difficult situations by denying the very possibility they exist in the first place. It can be pouring rain outside, but in her mom's mind all you have to do is say, *Rain, what rain?* and, *poof,* the rain is gone. The fact is, Kate may be jamming out right now in front of the mirror, pretending she's the greatest rock star who ever lived, and by asking for the guitar back, Flannery's going to ruin her whole Christmas Eve.

Outside, the light is already dimming, even though it's only a little after four. The sky is a pinkish gray, and it won't be long before the first star of the evening shows itself, a little silver dot that winks and blinks over the world. Flannery thinks she should go back into the house and get Rocko, so she can have a little company on her walk down the street, but then she pictures Rocko snoozing by the fireplace and figures it wouldn't be fair to wake him just so she won't feel lonely. Lately, the fur around his eyes has gotten whiter, and he's stopped chasing squirrels. Flannery has had Rocko since she was three, and it is hard to believe she won't always have him, but she knows he's getting old. He's already lived past the age the books say a bulldog will live. Maybe there's some sort of operation Rocko could have, Flannery thinks vaguely, not exactly able to say what the operation would be for. Immortality?

She looks back at her house, to see if Stan has turned the lights on yet. Flannery is not Stan the Man's biggest fan, but she has to admit he puts on an impressive Christmas light show. It is probably the best one in the neighborhood, but that might be because there are two families on their street where the parents always travel for work and never decorate anything, which cuts down the competition, and then there's that old lady with all the rose-bushes, whose house is always dark at night, like maybe she goes to bed at five or something. She is definitely not the type to put up Christmas lights.

Stan puts up his lights the day after Thanksgiving. Flannery knows her mom wishes that he would wait. Her mom is the sort of person who thinks you shouldn't get your Christmas tree until the week before Christmas. But Stan is not the sort of person who takes other people's opinions into consideration. He does things his way, because in his opinion, his way is the best and only way.

Flannery stoops to scoop up a handful of small white stones from somebody's rock garden. She wonders if you could get arrested for stealing rocks. It might make Christmas more interesting if she spent it in jail.

The problem with being thirteen, Flannery thinks, is that Christmas isn't that fun anymore. "Santa Claus" still visits her house, but what he brings is clothes Flannery's mom hopes like anything she'll wear (she won't) and a few books that a bookstore salesclerk has recommended for girls Flannery's age, and gloves and a new wallet, stuff like that. Flannery doesn't care. She doesn't even bother making a Christmas list anymore. She can get all the music she wants off the Internet, and music is pretty much all she cares about anyway.

There are a few lights on at the Fabers', so Flannery figures somebody is probably home. She gets a little excited thinking about her guitar and wonders why she's waited so long— since the beginning of school, she realizes—to ask for it back. It's not like she's been so busy studying. Flannery doesn't have to study very much, though her mom tells her that will change when she goes to high school. Flannery doubts it.

No, Flannery knows why she hasn't asked. Because her dad, Hawaii Bob as she's come to refer to him, promised her a new guitar last summer, when she'd had lunch with him at the airport. He had a layover of two hours, and he and Flannery had spent it at a crowded hamburger place, the floor littered with scrunched-up napkins and decimated French fries. That was the only time she'd seen him all year, but she figured the guitar would make up for the lack of real face time.

If she'd asked Kate for her old guitar back, it would be like admitting she didn't think the new guitar was coming. And Flannery believed it was. In fact, she could hear the rumbling of a UPS truck on the next block. Her guitar might be on it, sitting on the seat next to the driver, HANDLE WITH CARE scrawled across the box.

Flannery realizes as she rings the Fabers' doorbell that she is no longer holding the little white stones she's stolen. Turning around, she can barely make out a trail of them behind her, where she has dropped them one by one. Like she would need a trail to follow to get home, she thinks. Like getting back home is so important.

It is Christmas Eve, and Matthew Holler is sitting on the living-room couch watching *Frosty the Snowman* with his little sister. Sarah is addicted to Christmas specials, and she refuses to watch them by herself. His older sister, Carrie, took the early afternoon shift—*Rudolph the Red-Nosed Reindeer*, *Rudolph's Shiny New Year*, *The Little Drummer Boy*—and now it is Matthew's turn. He doesn't mind *Frosty the Snowman* so much, but he hates the other one that's on the same DVD, *Frosty and the Environmental Disaster*, something like that. It's a bunch of bull, in Matthew's opinion, just something they did so somebody could make a bunch of money.

People ruin everything, he thinks, at least the greed-heads do. They make sequels to shows that don't need sequels. There should only be one Rudolph story and one Frosty the Snowman story and one Charlie Brown Christmas story.

It occurs to Matthew that this is a pretty stupid conversation to be having with himself, but he can't help what he thinks about. The thoughts pretty much show up whether Matthew wants them to or not. Besides, he is bored with *Frosty the Snowman*, bored with sitting around the house, bored with Christmas. His parents are out making the rounds of Christmas open houses and won't be back until nine. Matthew, Carrie, and Sarah could have gone with them, but Matthew and Carrie didn't want to, and so Sarah didn't want to either. She is nine but considers herself to be Matthew and Carrie's equal, both socially and intellectually.

When the phone rings, Matthew jumps up to get it. He is not usually a phone guy, but suddenly he's hoping it's one of his friends, Sam, maybe, or Evan or Kate, anyone to talk to.

Maybe it's Kate, and she wants to play guitar over the phone. They do that now a few times a week, mostly just one playing, and then the other, but the other night they played a song together, a Pink Floyd song he'd learned from Sam called "Wish You Were Here." He even sang, which was not something he did a lot, not with other people, at least.

It's not Kate, however, or Sam or Evan. It's Emily. A thought darts through his mind that he's not quick enough to grab hold of, but it comes back a few seconds later, and this time he catches it: He is sorry it's Emily, not Kate, who has called him. Emily talks too much, for one thing, and what she has to say isn't all that interesting. Sure, she's hot, and no one's ever said Matthew Holler didn't have a thing for hot girls. But after a few weeks of hanging out, sometimes Matthew is filled with the desire to smash something when he hears Emily's voice, not because she makes him angry, but because he feels like it's a waste of time. Maybe hotness isn't everything, he thinks as Emily recites a list of what she wants for

Christmas. It's a high percentage of everything, just not 100 percent.

"Oh, yeah, hey, listen—there's my mom. I've gotta go." Matthew hangs up the phone before Emily even has a chance to say good-bye, which he realizes is a pretty harsh thing to do, especially on Christmas Eve, but if he stayed on the phone one more second, he is pretty sure his brain would have exploded.

Looking into the family room, he sees that Sarah is totally absorbed in the second *Frosty*, the one Matthew can't stand, so he sneaks upstairs to his room. It's a complete and impressive wreck, and he's supposed to have it cleaned up before his parents get back. Like what, they're going to cancel Christmas if his bed isn't made? He closes his door, grabs his guitar, and sits on the edge of his bed, working out the solo that comes in the middle of "Wish You Were Here." He could go online and print out a chart—there are only two hundred thousand Pink Floyd fan sites where you can find tabs and barre chords—but he'd rather do it himself.

He's almost got it worked out when his brain flips from "Wish You Were Here" to "God Rest Ye Merry Gentlemen," which has always been Matthew's favorite Christmas carol. Can you even play that on guitar? he wonders. He listens to it in his mind and then slowly starts translating the notes in his head to his guitar. E minor, he's pretty sure, then C, then B—no, B-7.

He gets it worked out, then plays through it a couple of times until he's happy with his strumming. It sounds good, he thinks, then looks around his room and thinks that playing Christmas carols by yourself is beside the point somehow. He suddenly imagines himself walking down the middle of his street, his guitar strapped on over his winter jacket, singing all the Christmas songs he knows. He can't help himself—he starts working out the chords to "Santa Claus Is Coming to Town," "O Little Town of Bethlehem," "Rudolph the Red-Nosed Reindeer."

You're not really going to do this, he tells himself as he's figuring whether "Frosty the

Snowman" starts out with a G or a C. There's no way.

Definitely no way would I ever do that, he thinks, standing up and looking around his room for his coat and the scarf his mom knitted him last Christmas. That is so completely not what I'm about.

He is careful to not let the screen door slam behind him as he sneaks out of the house and heads toward the road.

It is Christmas Eve, and Kate is trying to string popcorn, which turns out to be an amazingly hard thing to do. The only reason she's doing it is that her mom and dad had this big, nostalgic conversation at lunch, about how they were too poor to afford ornaments for their bare, scraggly tree their first Christmas as a married couple; all they had to decorate it with was long strands of popcorn, which made the tree look like it was covered with freshly fallen snow.

So now Kate is stuck trying to run a needle threaded with dental floss through piece after piece of microwave popcorn. So far she has gotten six pieces on the floss and destroyed seventeen. It is, she thinks, a losing battle, but she can tell it makes her mom happy that she's trying, and since Kate is not sure her mom will like Kate's Christmas present to her, she figures this could be a kind of present too.

When the doorbell rings, Kate jumps up to get it. "Anything to stop stringing popcorn" is becoming her motto of the day. She thinks it is probably the UPS man, since she just heard the truck out on the road, and the presents from her Uncle Simon and Aunt Kim still haven't arrived, even though Aunt Kim swore up and down on the phone to Kate's mom that she'd mailed them a week ago.

Instead, it's Flannery. "Bad news," Flannery says the second the door is open. "I have to take my guitar back."

Adrenaline surges through Kate's stomach and up and down her legs. She realizes she has pretty much forgotten that her guitar is actually Flannery's guitar. When Flannery first lent it to her at the end of the summer, Kate had thought a lot about how she could save up money for her own guitar, but after weeks, then months went by, and Flannery never asked for her guitar back, Kate had sort of convinced herself that Flannery didn't actually want it back.

"Come on in," she says to Flannery now. "I'll go get it."

Flannery follows Kate to her room. "I'm probably getting a new guitar for Christmas from my dad," she says, "so if it was up to me I'd let you keep it. But my stepbrother's here, and he lost his guitar on the plane, and apparently he can't live without a guitar in his hands every minute of the day."

"How'd he lose it on the plane?" Kate asks as she pulls the guitar case out of the closet. The guitar itself is on a stand next to her bed.

"Not on the plane. I mean all of his luggage got lost, including his guitar. They think it's probably in Atlanta. The fact is, he's a terrible guitar player. I don't know why everyone's acting like if he doesn't have a guitar to play, the world will be deprived of his great talent.

Believe me, we'd be better off if no one let him near a guitar ever again."

Kate is careful as she lays the guitar in its case. She wonders what she'll do without her guitar. Without Flannery's guitar. She was going to spend her whole vacation writing new songs, maybe even recording some. Matthew said that he might be able to get them into the audio lab over Christmas, that the audio lab director, Mr. Norris, was going to open it up a few hours a day for anybody who was interested. They were going to try to record something together, just for fun. But she isn't going to be able to record anything without a guitar.

Worse, she realizes suddenly, she isn't going to be able to give her mom her Christmas present. Every year Kate's mom said, "Don't buy me something for Christmas, make me something," and every year Kate and Tracie went to Target and bought something their mom totally didn't need, electric coffee grinders and rice steamers, fancy little soaps for the downstairs bathroom. But finally, this year, Kate has actually made something. She's written her mom a song.

A word springs into Kate's head. It is a word she isn't supposed to say, a word she's never heard her mom say, and has only heard her dad say a few times, when he was driving in bad traffic. Kate says it now, under her breath at first, and then louder, and then four times in a row.

And then, to her embarrassment, she starts to cry. "Sorry," she apologizes to Flannery. "I just, well, I was going to a play a song on it. I mean, for my mom, in the morning. For a present. I didn't really get her anything else."

Flannery looks at her a long time without saying anything, and Kate feels like an idiot. It is Marylin who understands about moms and Christmas presents. Kate has come to believe that Flannery is a decent human being, but that doesn't mean she is sentimental or actually cares about what Kate's mom gets for Christmas.

To Kate's surprise, Flannery shrugs. "Hey, that's cool. Ellis can play the guitar my dad's sending me for Christmas. The UPS guy is probably dropping it off right now. I kind of hate to let Ellis get his grimy little paws on it,

221

but he's only here three more days."

Kate does not hug Flannery. She does not sob grateful tears of joy. She knows that she has exceeded the limits of Flannery's tolerance for emotional displays already with her crying. So all she does is say, "Thanks." And then, "You don't happen to want to string some popcorn with me, do you?"

Flannery shrugs again. "Okay, yeah, sure. I could use some big excitement in my life right now. Besides, anything's better than hanging out with Ellis."

Just as Kate's settled into her seat and picked up her strand of mutilated popcorn, the doorbell rings, and she is saved again. It is the UPS man, with two big boxes—one from Uncle Simon and Aunt Kim—and the other, a long, flat box, from the Guitar Center. Kate's mom rushes up behind her.

"I'll get those, honey, you just run along!" she says, clearly trying to sound nonchalant. She pokes her head out the door and calls, "Thanks! Merry Christmas!" to the retreating UPS man. Then she says to Kate, "Oh, honey, I forgot to check the mail today; run and get it, would you?"

Kate walks down the driveway to the mailbox. She waves to the UPS man as he drives in the direction of Flannery's house. She waits for the truck to stop, so she can watch the UPS man carry Flannery's guitar up to the front door. She thinks it would be nice to go back into the kitchen and say, "Hey, Flannery, guess what! I think your guitar has arrived!" It can be like a little present she gives Flannery, in exchange for the present Flannery has given her.

But the UPS truck does not stop in front of Flannery's house. It lumbers down the street and turns left onto Sagebrush Drive.

When Kate returns to the kitchen, she doesn't say anything about the UPS truck or guitars. She just picks up her needle and begins her attack on the popcorn. When she glances over at Flannery, Kate is amazed to see that Flannery has already strung two feet of dental floss. "That's amazing," she says. "How did you get so good at that?"

"I was a Brownie in third grade," Flannery

replies, "and my Brownie leader was totally into stringing popcorn. We did it for, like, three weeks in a row. I was the champ."

"You were a Brownie?" Kate asks. Of course, what she wants to ask is, *They let people like you in Brownies?* but it's Christmas Eve, so she doesn't.

Flannery grins. "I was an amazing Brownie." She looks up from her popcorn. "You might not know this, but I was a really nice little kid."

"Pretty hard to believe," Kate jokes, and Flannery throws a piece of popcorn at her. Kate pops it into her mouth. She plucks another piece of popcorn from the bowl and pokes her needle at it. The fact is, she can believe that Flannery was a nice kid. About 90 percent of people are nice kids up through second grade, and then the percentages start to dip. By sixth grade, it's probably down to 40 percent. A picture of Mazie Calloway pops into her head, and Kate revises her estimate to 30 percent.

But maybe things get better, Kate thinks, glancing up at Flannery, whose face is squinched in concentration, like the only thing that matters at this very minute is guiding that needle through the popcorn. Maybe even Mazie Calloway will turn nice one day.

Okay, Kate actually doubts that Mazie Calloway will ever be anything besides a horrible human being. But it's Christmas, and she is in the mood to feel hopeful about everything.

Especially about that long, flat box with the Guitar Center return address.

Kate is very hopeful about that.

It is Christmas Eve, and Marylin is putting eyeliner on an angel. "Hold still, sweetie," she says, and tries to remember what Rhetta has told her about applying eye makeup. Smudged lines are better than thin, sharp lines. You are creating shadows and light. Subtle is good. No clown faces.

Marylin thinks she's sort of good at this. Not as good as Rhetta, who right now is transforming the girl playing the Virgin Mary from a pale, slightly cross-eyed ten-year-old into the serene, graceful-looking mother of Jesus. *Makeup is magic* is another thing Rhetta likes to say, and Marylin is starting to believe it.

Reverend Mayes sweeps through the room, looking strange to Marylin in his white robe. She has gone to church twice with Rhetta, and both times Reverend Mayes was dressed in a polo shirt and chinos. He is the most laid-back minister Marylin has ever met. But now he looks a little nervous, like if this Christmas pageant's a flop, God might get mad at him.

"I see only two wise men," he says, surveying the room, which is filled with sheep, shepherds, angels, and various farm animals. "Where's the third one?"

"Owen is sick," a sheep calls from the corner. "I forgot his mom said for me to tell you that. He has a cold and maybe strep, only she couldn't get an appointment to find out, so she was going to take him this afternoon to Urgent Care over by the Food Lion so he—"

Reverend Mayes cuts the sheep off. "Thanks, Seth, I think I get it." He turns to a thin woman who is busy hemming an angel's robe. "So who can we get to substitute, Lisa? Any ideas? It'll look strange to just have two wise men."

The woman looks around the room. "How about Rhetta?"

Rhetta holds up her hands, like she's trying to keep that idea from landing on her. "I'm strictly behind the scenes, Dad. We've talked about that."

"But it's an emergency, honey. Help me out here."

Rhetta looks over at Marylin, and Marylin shakes her head no. It's not that she's afraid of standing up in front of crowds. As a middle-school cheerleader, she does it all the time. But she has never stood in front of a bunch of people trying to look, well, holy. She doesn't think she can pull it off.

Reverend Mayes catches the look between Rhetta and Marylin and smiles. "Marylin! You'd be an awesome wise man—or wise woman, if you prefer. Do me this favor, sweetheart. It would mean so much to all these children, who have worked so hard to put together a nice pageant."

Well, how are you supposed to refuse a minister? How is Marylin supposed to say no to all these little lambs and angels? So she lets Rhetta put a humongous crown on her head and drape her in a red velvet robe lined with fake leopard skin. One look in the mirror and Marylin knows she looks ridiculous, but she supposes it's for a good cause. Besides, it's not like anyone from school besides Rhetta will be there.

When it is the three wise men's turn, they march down the aisle of the church singing, "We Three Kings." Fortunately, Marylin knows all the words, even from the second and third verses. She tries to remember to sing loudly, but she is pretty caught up in keeping the gold coins from falling off the pillow she is carrying. With every step, they slide a little closer to the edge of the pillow, and Marylin thinks if she doesn't get to the baby Jesus soon, those coins are going to fall off and roll down to the altar.

Sure enough, when the wise men come to a stop, one of the coin slips off the pillow and onto the floor, but looking around, Marylin doesn't think anyone has noticed. They're all too busy oohing and aahing at the baby Jesus, who is a real baby, a girl with blond, wispy hair. The baby Jesus is looking around and smiling at everyone, and Marylin can tell this is making people happy by the way they are making little cooing sounds.

After she has set down the pillow in front of baby Jesus's straw bed, Marylin stands up, relieved to be done with her part. She realizes she hasn't seen her parents and Petey yet. In fact, she has sort of forgotten they'd be here. This isn't their church, after all, not that they've gone to any church very much in the past year. If she hadn't agreed to help Rhetta with the Christmas pageant, Marylin and Petey would already be at her dad's apartment, miles away from any church Marylin could think of.

She scans the pews, expecting to find her father on one side of the aisle and her mother on the other, but no, there they are, all together, slightly toward the back of the church, with

Petey scrunched between them. She catches her mom's eye, and her mom waves at her, then taps her dad on the shoulder, as if to tell him, *Hey, Marylin sees us!* Her dad's face lights up in a grin, and he waves a little half wave. Marylin waves the tiniest wave back.

After the pageant, Marylin introduces her parents to Reverend Mayes, who shakes her dad's hand and says, "Call me Jack. Marylin was a lifesaver tonight. She's a great kid."

Her parents beam. "Yeah, she is," her dad says, and her mom nods her head in agreement.

"Come visit us some Sunday," Reverend Mayes says to them. "I know you two . . . I know you're not together anymore, but, hey, as long as you've got these two fine kids here, you'll always be family."

Marylin's mom tears up a little. Marylin's dad shakes Reverend Mayes's hand again, says thanks, and the four of them walk out to the parking lot.

"Not bad, for church," her dad says. "He

seems like an all right guy. Strange-looking daughter, though." He reaches into his pocket for his car keys. "That's the girl you're such big friends with all the sudden?" he asks Marylin.

"We're sort of friends," Marylin says. "I mean, yeah, we're friends. She's much more normal than she looks."

Marylin's parents have parked next to each other. Marylin is opening the door to her dad's car when Petey yells, "Oh, no! I forgot something! Something important!"

"What did you forget, honey?" Marylin's mom asks. "Your pj's?"

Petey looks sheepish. Marylin can tell he doesn't want to say. "I forgot my notebook," he mumbles. "It's, uh, for science. And I really need it."

Marylin's dad checks his watch. "We really need to be heading out, kiddo," he says. "My plan was to order Chinese tonight, and if we don't get back to my place soon, it's going to be eight before we eat."

"Dad, you don't understand," Petey pleads. "I need that notebook. It's got equations in it. I can't explain it. But it's kind of a Christmas project."

Marylin's mom puts her arm around Petey's shoulder. "Why don't we go back to the house and have dinner there? We'll order some pizza, Petey can get his notebook, and you all can hit the road."

Please say yes, please say yes, Marylin thinks, crossing her fingers. She wants her family to eat pizza together on Christmas Eve. She wants one thing about this Christmas to be almost normal. She looks up in the sky and finds an especially bright star to make a wish on. I promise I won't think my parents are getting back together, she tells the star. I promise I know we're not all going to show up at church as a family on Sunday. Just let me have this one thing.

The star seems to wink at Marylin, and then it shines a little brighter in the cold air. She closes her eyes and waits.

"That sounds like a good plan," Marylin's dad says after a long pause. "I'll follow you over to the house in my car."

When they pull into the driveway, Marylin hops out of the minivan. She feels like dancing across the lawn, even imagines she hears Christmas music in the air.

And then she realizes that she does, in fact, hear Christmas music in the air.

"Where's that coming from?" her mom asks, getting out of the van. "It's beautiful."

That's when Marylin sees it, someone standing in Kate's driveway. It is a boy with a guitar, and he's singing "Silent Night."

"It's him," Marylin says, pointing to the boy. She takes a few steps toward Kate's house. She wants to get closer, see who it is. Just then, the Fabers' front door opens, and Kate walks outside, followed by somebody else—Flannery? How strange, Marylin thinks. Both girls appear to be carrying guitars.

Petey grabs Marylin by the hand. "Christmas caroling! Come on, Marylin!" He pulls her in the direction of Kate's house. "We'll be right back," he calls to his parents.

"Five minutes!" his dad calls back, like he still lives at their house, like he's still the boss of it.

Marylin and Petey cross the street and run across the lawns to Kate's house, holding hands and laughing, and when they get there, they start to sing, without even bothering to say hello, without bothering to ask if they can, just joining in, because it is Christmas Eve, and everybody is welcome.

Looking for more Kate and Marylin?
Turn the page to read the beginning
of *The Secret Language of Girls*!

what would you trade?

"Do you think bugs have dreams?" Kate asked Marylin, nudging a rock with her foot. A mob of roly-polies scurried toward the sidewalk in a state of panic.

"I don't think bugs even have brains," Marylin said, pulling her knees to her chest so the roly-polies couldn't crawl up her legs. "I wouldn't touch those if I were you," she added. "They might carry really gross diseases."

Too late. Kate was jabbing roly-poly after roly-poly with her finger to get them to curl into tiny balls. She scooped up a bunch of the silvery bugs and watched them roll around in the palm of her hand. "Yum," Kate said. "Want some peas for dinner?"

It was at times like these that Marylin thought Kate still had some growing up to do.

A lightning bug flashed a few feet away from where Marylin and Kate were sitting on the front steps of Kate's house, and then the evening sky dimmed just a notch and suddenly the yard was filled with lightning bugs. According to Marylin's little brother, Petey, when lightning bugs flashed their lights, they were sending signals to each other. *Here I am*, they were saying. *Have I told you lately that I love you?*

Kate was up and running. She swooped like a bird every time a lightning bug flashed in her path, using her cupped palm like a small butterfly net to nab one bug after another. The sky dimmed another notch, and now Kate's tanned legs looked white as paper, as though she'd turned into a ghost. Marylin could see Kate's bare feet glowing like two little moons as she ran through the damp grass.

"Okay, let's see here," Kate said, walking back to the steps, her hands trapping the flashing lights, red glowing through her fingers. She peeked through the small crack between her thumbs. "I count six, no, seven lightning bugs. What would you trade for seven lightning bugs?" she asked Marylin.

What would you trade? It was the game Kate and Marylin had been playing ever since the beginning of nursery school, when Marylin had moved into the house five mailboxes down on the other side of the street. What would you trade for my peanut butter sandwich? My Mickey Mouse ears? For seventeen Pixy Stix?

Marylin dug into her pocket and pulled out half a stick of Juicy Fruit gum. She held it out to Kate.

"No trade," Kate said. "I'm not allowed to chew gum unless it's sugar free."

"That's all I've got," Marylin said. "Take it or leave it."

Kate opened her palms to the humid air and watched the lightning bugs flutter away into the dark. "I guess we shouldn't trade living things, anyway."

The porch light flickered on. Marylin stuck out her leg in front of her and examined her foot. "How about toes? I'd trade toes with you."

Marylin thought her toes were her worst feature. She couldn't believe she had never noticed how weird her toes were until Matthew Sholls had pointed it out to her at the swimming pool the day before. Her second toes were longer than her big toes, and her little toes barely existed. All the rest of her toes were sort of crooked. Kate had perfectly normal, straight toes. Her big toes were the longest, just like they were supposed to be. Kate's little toes were like two plump peanuts.

Kate sat down next to Marylin. "Toes? Who cares about toes?"

Marylin faked a laugh. "Yeah, I know, it's pretty dumb. You're right. Who cares about toes?"

"Come on," Kate said. "Let's go see what's on TV."

Marylin followed Kate inside. The air-conditioning hummed a steady stream of cool air through the house. Marylin shivered a little as she and Kate made their way down the stairs to the basement TV room. She should have brought a sweater with her. She should have brought some socks to cover up her crooked toes.

As much as Marylin hated to, she had to admit it: She was the sort of person who cared about toes.

In three weeks Marylin and Kate would begin sixth grade. The idea of starting middle school made Marylin's stomach go icy cold, like she'd swallowed a cupful of snow. She thought it was possible she would start having boyfriends in sixth grade. A lot of girls she knew had boyfriends. It was a very normal thing to do.

The fact was, Marylin hadn't officially talked to a boy since she'd punched Dale Morrell in the nose in fourth grade. Boys made her nervous, and Marylin preferred to avoid nervous-making situations. But according to the books on puberty her mom had given her last week, any second now she could be chasing Dale Morrell through the hallways of Brenner P. Dunn Middle School trying to make him kiss her. Marylin had known some fifth-grade girls who had done that. Brittany Lamb was practically famous for it. It was the sort of thing Kate couldn't stand. Kate hated kissing of all kinds.

Marylin had mixed opinions about kissing. She liked it when her dad kissed her on the nose at bedtime, but she hated being kissed by Grandma McIntosh, whose kisses left gooey, fuchsia lipstick prints on Marylin's cheek. As for kissing boys, well, Marylin just didn't know. If they were movie stars, sure. Marylin had already spent a lot of time imagining kissing movie stars. But in real life Marylin didn't know any movie stars. She knew boys like Matthew Sholls and Dale Morrell. They were not the kind of people who inspired her to dreams of kissing.

Before going over to Kate's house, Marylin had been sitting on her bed, pulling her left foot as close to her head as possible so she could examine her toes, when her mother had walked into the room and flopped down next to her.

"Mom, do you think my toes would look normal if I put nail polish on them?" Marylin asked. She wiggled her toes so her mom could take in the full effect of their weirdness.

"You have wonderful toes!" Marylin's mom exclaimed. "You have my aunt Bette's toes. Everyone loved Aunt Bette."

"Yeah, but did everyone love her toes?"

"What is this toe obsession of yours, Shnooks?" Marylin's mom put on her I'm-a-concerned-mother-and-I'm-here-to-help face, which Marylin liked a lot better than the leave-me-alone-I've-just-had-a-fight-with-your-father face she'd been wearing earlier in the afternoon, right after Marylin's dad had left on another business trip. Marylin tried not to think about the fight or the trip or the fact that she had to spend the night at Kate's tonight so her mom could call up Aunt Tish and complain about her dad. She'd rather think about toes.

"I don't want to miss out on any of life's big opportunities because of my toes," Marylin explained. "Am I too young for plastic surgery?"

That was when her mom talked to her for a long time about boys and how, no matter what, Marylin was not to pull any stupid beauty stunts to get boys to like her, like bleach her hair platinum blond or pluck off all her eyebrows or get plastic surgery on her toes. And makeup was definitely out. Marylin's mom was famous for being against eleven-year-old girls wearing makeup. It was one of her favorite topics of discussion.

"You're a very pretty girl, Marylin," her mom insisted. "People pay to have hair like yours— it's like moonlight. And brown eyes? Please! Don't ruin what nature's given you."

"But what about nail polish, Mom?" Marylin asked when her mom was through. "Nail polish isn't really makeup."

Her mom considered this for a moment. Ever since she and Marylin's dad had been fighting so much, you could sometimes get her to change her mind about things. It was like she had only so much fighting energy in her. "No black," she said finally, giving Marylin a stern look. "I absolutely forbid black."

"No black," Marylin had promised.

"So when did you start painting your toenails, anyway?" Kate asked Marylin during a commercial break. "I can't believe your mom would let you do that."

"She said it was okay," Marylin said, wiggling her toes so they shimmered a little in the TV's blue glow. "I just can't use black or purple or anything like that. My mom said pink is perfectly respectable."

"Whatever," Kate said, turning back to the TV, where a glamorous woman was shaking her head around so that her hair bounced up and down like a Slinky. The woman was wearing a long, silky dress that was cut low in the front. Watching her made Marylin feel itchy. She wondered what the glamorous woman's parents thought when they saw her on tele-vision. Did they wish she'd covered up a little more?

Marylin picked up a pen and a pad of paper from the coffee table. Lately she'd been prac-ticing her signature, trying to make it look more sophisticated. Who knew—maybe she'd be a movie star one day and would have to sign autographs left and right. A few weeks ago she'd changed the spelling of her name from Marilyn to Marylin, to make it seem less old-fashioned. How her parents had come up with the idea of naming a girl born on the very brink of the twenty-first century *Marilyn* was beyond her.

"Who's 'Marylin'?" Kate asked, peering over Marylin's shoulder. "Did you know you were spelling your own name wrong?"

"This is how I spell my name now," Marylin explained. "It's the new me."

"Why do you need to be a new you?" Kate

wanted to know. "There's nothing wrong with the old you. I like the old you."

"I'm sick of the old me," Marylin said. She hadn't realized this until she said it out loud, but she instantly knew it was the truth.

Sounds of distress from the kitchen suddenly tumbled down the stairs. "Scram! Go on now!!" Kate's mom cried. "Get away from there, you dumb cat!"

Kate jumped up. "What's wrong, Mom?" she called, running to the stairs.

"Oh, there's this stupid cat—" Mrs. Faber's voice broke off. Marylin could hear her pounding on the window. "Stop that! Stop that!"

Kate flew up the steps, Marylin following close on her heels. When they reached the kitchen, Mrs. Faber was out in the yard chasing an orange cat with a bird in its mouth.

"Drop it, you stupid animal!" Mrs. Faber yelled after the cat as it disappeared in the dark border of the boxwood shrubs. She turned to Kate and Marylin, who had joined her in the yard. "This is why we have a dog," she said angrily. "Dogs don't eat birds."

"Don't you remember that time Max tried to eat a duck?" Kate asked her mom. Max was the Fabers' basset hound.

"Max wasn't trying to eat the duck," Mrs. Faber said, sounding irritated. "He was trying to smell it. That's what basset hounds do. They smell things."

Marylin heard a peeping noise from the bushes in front of the Fabers' screened porch. She followed the peeps until she found a nest perched on a tight canopy of branches illuminated by the porch light. In the nest was a tiny gray bird with its mouth opened so wide, Marylin could see all the way down its throat.

"It's waiting for its mom to come back to feed it," Kate said, coming up behind Marylin. "It looks really hungry."

"I don't think its mom is coming back," Mrs. Faber said. She patted Kate's shoulder. "I think the cat got its mom."

"I guess we'll have to feed it, then," Kate said. "We'll put its nest in a shoe box and keep it inside, where it can be warm at night. We'll find it some worms."

"It probably won't make it, Kate," Mrs. Faber said. She sounded sad. "I don't think the little bird will make it without its mom."

Kate ignored her mother. Turning to Marylin, she said, "Go get Petey. He can help us dig up worms. Tell him to bring a flashlight. And ask your mom if she has an eyedropper. We'll need an eyedropper."

Marylin felt like a soldier taking orders from General Patton. "Yes, sir!" she said to Kate, and then she turned and ran through the damp grass toward home, wondering when Kate had suddenly become boss of the world.